GU00731344

JOHNNY NOTHING
Ian Probert

First published in Great Britain by Ian Probert, 2014
Copyright © Ian Probert, 2014
This book is copyright under the Berne
Convention. No reproduction without permission.
® And © Ian Probert. All rights reserved.
The right of Ian Probert to be identified as author of this
work has been asserted in accordance with sections 77
and 78 of the Copyright, Designs and Patents Act, 1988.
www.ianprobert.com
A CIP catalogue record for this book
is available from the British Library
ISBN-13: 978-1500670139
ISBN-10: 1500670138

To my amazing wife Laura and my beautiful and talented daughter Sofia, whose drawings inspired this story.

Contents

Contents

Prologue

Parents – I'm sure you'll agree – are very different to you. They sprout hair in **RIDICULOUS** places. They shed hair in others. They have bizarre, flabby, bobbly bits that wobble about in slow motion when they run. They leave absolutely **HORRENDOUS**, unspeakable stinks in the bathroom that make you **GAG**.

They cover the sink with bristles. They own hundreds of bottles of weird coloured liquids that they drink or swallow or inhale or stick up their bottoms. They smother their faces in gloopy cream that they think makes them look younger but in fact makes them look exactly the same age as before only smothered in gloopy cream. They definitely come from another planet – a pretty rancid one at that.

They are also contrary creatures. They say one thing and do another.

They put you to bed early but stay up late. They forbid you

to eat sweets and then fill their fat, greasy faces with chocolate as soon as you're not looking. They order you not to swear and then curse at the TV when Simon Cowell comes on. They demand you are careful with the pitiful amount of pocket money that they give you and then pack the house with stupid electronic gadgets or handbags or shoes that cost a **DISGUSTING** amount of money.

This is the story of the worst parent of all time: the meanest, nastiest, smelliest, ugliest, sweatiest mother you could possibly imagine. Even worse than your own, in fact. And it's the story of what she did to her son, who's really very nice actually. Probably a lot nicer than you are.

If you ever think that you're hard done by. If you've ever wished that you could trade your boring parents in or sell them on eBay or something then you're in for a shock. Because by the time you've gotten to know Felicity MacKenzie you're going to think you have the best parents in the world…

Chapter 01 – Dead

Everybody looked so **BORED**.

The bloke playing the organ looked **BORED**. The bloke with his shirt on the wrong way round looked **BORED**. The people sitting on wooden benches staring at really hopeless poetry looked **BORED**. The windows looked **BORED**. The doors looked **BORED**. The whole world was just **BORED**. But Johnny Nothing was having the time of his life.

No, it's a lie actually – he was **BORED** too. **BORED** out of his brain.

'Who's Johnny Nothing and why is everybody **BORED**?' I hear you say.

Well... Johnny Nothing is a ten-year-old boy, probably about the same age as you are. (Unless you're one of those dreadful precocious spotty little brats who pretend that they can read books written for older people and secretly can't.) He's average looking. Average height. Average hair... In fact, let's save our-selves a little time shall we? Here's a picture of him:

He doesn't look very happy, does he? Well nor would you if you had the kind of thoroughly rotten time that he does. But before I tell you all about this I think you'll agree that he's nothing much to look at. He's like any one of a number of boys that go to your school. Sometimes he's naughty. Sometimes he's good. Some-times he lies. Sometimes he tells the truth. He's not over-clever. He's not under-stupid.

If Johnny was a colour he wouldn't be yellow or red or blue or green or violet or gold or silver. He'd just be grey. Dull, muddy, grey. If he was a sound he'd be a monotonous drone. If he was a smell he'd be the smell of nothingness.

He's someone who doesn't stand out from the crowd. Some-one who is one of the last people chosen when you're picking sides for a game of footy in the playground. Someone whom clever parents with posh accents might call 'unremarkable'. Am I making myself clear? Johnny's just ordinary.

Just ordinary, except for one thing which I'll tell you about on page 4[1] because right now I've got to get back to explaining why everybody was **BORED**.

Everybody was **BORED** because it was the day of Uncle Marley's funeral. And let me tell you this: funerals are just about the most tiresome, dreary occasions in the whole wide universe. Anyone who has ever been to one is guaranteed to agree with me. They're dull as dishwater. They're stinky as a fridgeful of rancid foreign cheese. They're a complete waste of time. That's why you'll never hear anyone say: 'Went to a totally brilliant funeral the other day. It was fantastic. I've never laughed so much in my life. Can't wait for the sequel…'

If I had my way I'd ban funerals. When people die you should be allowed to put them in a black plastic sack and leave them out for the bin men to collect. Or you should be allowed to chuck them into the nearest canal so that they get washed out to sea and eventually end up on a beach somewhere in France. Let the French deal with the problem.

But no. Instead we give our dead to an undertaker, who tries to make the body look less dead by caking its face in make-up and slapping on a bit of lippy. He then crams its mouth full of cotton wool and sticks the body in a really expensive wooden crate that is then either:

---

1   If this is the iBooks version of Johnny Nothing that you're reading then I really have no idea what page it's on.

a/ burned to a cinder in a huge oven
b/ buried in a hole in the ground where it is slowly eaten by worms
c/ what I mean about letting the French deal with the problem?

Uncle Marley was currently in the make-up, lippy and cotton wool stage. He lay in a coffin positioned at the front of a large church, deep in dead man thought. Patiently waiting for all the boring speeches to come to an end so that he could be dropped into a hole in the ground and forgotten about.

If you've never seen a dead body before I should tell you one thing about them: they really are **DEAD**. They don't move. They don't twitch. They don't sneeze. They don't bottom-burp.[2] They just lie there looking dead. Uncle Marley was no exception. He was dead. He couldn't move a muscle even if he'd wanted to. It was as if somebody had hit the pause button on Sky Plus and then gone off on a really long holiday. That's a picture of Uncle Marley on the next page. Ugly isn't he?

One more thing: Dead people smell a lot, too. And unless you're reading the special scratch 'n' sniff version of this book there's simply no way that the picture above can do justice to the truly **HORRENDOUS** stink that was coming from Uncle Marley.

Do you know that wonderful aroma that you get on a Sunday afternoon when your mum is just about to slide the Sunday roast out of the oven and carve it into succulent slices? Or the

---

2   Although actually this isn't true because dead people have been known to produce truly horrendous, putrid farts that often cause the undertaker to bring up his breakfast.

sweet scent of blossom dancing in the air on a hot Summer's day as you eat a lovely cool ice cream with a dribble of raspberry sauce on top? Well Uncle Marley smelt like neither of those.

The odour that came from the corpse of Uncle Marley was... Well, imagine you've gone out into your street and accidentally stepped in some dog poo, and then scraped the dog poo off the bottom of your shoe and put it in your mum's smoothie maker with some cat sick and then hit the 'on' button and waited for twenty years. Well Uncle Marley smelt much, much worse than that. And yet strangely enough, nobody sitting in that decrepit old church even mentioned the absolutely **DISGUSTING** smell that Uncle Marley was producing.

Enough of talking about smells. Back to what's happening with the story:

'Blah... blah... blah... blah... Cleaned his teeth at least twice a week. Blah... blah... blah... blah... Never forgot his own birthday… Blah, blah, blah, blah… Changed his underpants once a month…' The bloke with his shirt on the wrong way round (from this point on we'll call him the vicar, shall we?) was giving his eulogy.

I think it's wrong to expect you to know what a eulogy is so I'll tell you: at a funeral it's a really bottom licking speech that is made about the person who's dead. It's usually given by a family member or a close personal friend. Or in this case a vicar. As you might imagine, eulogies are generally quite flattering speeches. People giving them usually concentrate on the deceased's good points rather than highlighting the bad.

For this reason, the vicar was making Uncle Marley sound like he was Santa Claus' less well-known but infinitely more generous younger brother. When in fact, if you could have hypnotised the vicar so that he was only allowed to tell the truth, this is what Uncle Marley's eulogy might have sounded like:

'Here lies the body of Jake Marley. An ugly old man with very bad breath and a completely **RIDICULOUS** wig. Mr. Marley spent most of his life drinking beer, eating chips, doing no exercise and being very nasty to small children… He never went to church, so quite why I'm giving this eulogy is a mystery to me… Everybody who knew him hated him and if it wasn't for the fact that he was a very, very, very, very, very, very, very, very, very, very, very, very, very, very[3] rich multi-millionaire he wouldn't have had a friend in the world. Good riddance Jake Marley, have a very unpleasant time dead and I hope that you go to Hell… PS You had BO.'

3　　In other words very

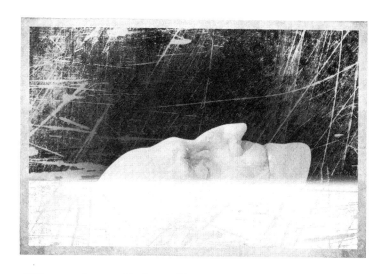

Chapter 02 - Funeral

Hello again. Glad that you could make it to Chapter Two. I really feel like we're getting somewhere now, don't you?

In no time at all we've established that there's a funeral going on. That it's boring (I've stopped using capitals for 'boring' now, it was getting **TEDIOUS**). That Uncle Marley is the corpse being placed in a hole in the ground. That Uncle Marley was **REALLY** rich. That Uncle Marley used to be horrible and mean and smelly when he was alive. That Uncle Marley is even more smelly but not quite so horrible and mean now that he's dead. And that Johnny Nothing is the hero of this story and that he's alive but pretty dull and ordinary. (except for one thing that I'm going to tell you about on page 4.)[4]

---

4   I've told you before! If this is the iBooks version of Johnny Nothing that you're reading then I really have no idea what page it's on.

Before I do that, it's time for a little background info about the other people attending the funeral. I think I'll start with the least important characters and then build up to the most important. Always a good idea, wouldn't you say?

OK. The first thing you should know is that because Uncle Marley was a rich and vile old Scroogeypants there weren't really a lot of mourners present at his funeral. In fact, there was nobody there that you could really call a friend because Uncle Marley had no friends. He just had money. Lots and lots of it. Indeed, there were only seven people present that morning and four of them were family members.

The organist

First of all, there was the bloke playing the organ. (I'll be honest with you: I don't actually know his name and he doesn't really have much to do with this story. I'm only really mentioning him because it would be rude not to.)

The Vicar

Then there was the vicar, who also doesn't really figure much in this story but will reappear if you like this book and purchase Book 2 in the series. I can, however, tell you that he was from Scotland and that his name was John McVicar. A bit of a coincidence him being a vicar and a having surname like McVicar, don't you think? But then again I used to have a headmaster called Ed Master and a gym teacher named Jim Teacher. So these types of coincidences are not actually that unusual.

Uncle Sydney

The next one worth mentioning is Uncle Sydney. He was Uncle Marley's younger brother and so incredibly nondescript that we've only hired him to appear in the first five chapters of this book. When he was at school he was more concerned with girls and with smoking cigarettes than concentrating on his school work. For this reason, although he has no job and his five ex-wives have run off with whatever money he once had, he does have a very loud and unhealthy sounding smoker's cough (don't smoke kids!). Sydney couldn't remember the last time that he had seen his brother and really couldn't care less that he was dead. He just wanted to know how much money he was going to get when this **BORING** funeral was over. (Sorry about that one – I accidentally had CAPS LOCK turned on.)

Billy MacKenzie

The next most important character in the story is probably Billy Mackenzie. Billy is Johnny's dad and Uncle Marley's brother-in-law, in view of the fact that he had the extreme misfortune to be married to Uncle Marley's sister. Billy lived in mortal fear of his wife. You'll meet her in a moment.

Imagine if an alien landed on our planet and the first person he bumped into was Billy MacKenzie. After spending a couple of minutes with Billy, the alien would conclude that our species was powered by gas. That's because Billy was one of those grown-ups who couldn't stop himself from producing gallons of mouldy methane. If it wasn't coming from his mouth in the form or big fruity burps, it was coming from his bottom with a smell like a blocked drain or an egg sandwich that someone is eating in the seat next to you on the train. And like a lot of grown-ups Billy thought that he was extremely clever whenever he produced one of these rancid stinks. As if he had discovered the cure for cancer and simultaneously solved world starvation.

Ebenezer Dark

Next in line is Ebenezer Dark. He was Uncle Marley's solicitor. He was in charge of making sure that Uncle Marley paid as little income tax as possible, as well as other duties, including making tea, killing people, going to the shops and the reading of Uncle Marley's will (before anyone asks, it's due to happen this very afternoon, as soon as the funeral is over). As the old saying goes, where there's a will there's a solicitor.

In case you didn't know, solicitors nearly always wear suits when they're soliciting. Mr. Dark was wearing quite an expensive suit and had slicked back hair that was perched on top of a body shaped like a black plastic sack full of melted lard. He looked how James Bond might look like if he lived on meat and potato pies and worked for the council and had a licence to read legal documents.

Nobody else there had ever met Mr. Dark before and they all looked at him suspiciously and said nasty things about him when he was out of earshot. When he was in earshot they smiled sweetly and said nice things about him just like some of your fiends do about you. (Sometimes you make mistakes when you're typing. I've left that last one in.)

Uncle Marley

Which leads us nicely on to Uncle Marley (that's him right at the start of this chapter). As we discussed earlier, he was currently lying pretty motionless in a wooden box gazing intently at the roof of the church as if it was the last thing in the world he would ever see. This was almost definitely true.

Until he had decided to take a permanent break from living, Jacob Ermentrude Marley was the 296th richest person in the UK. (Currently he was at number one in the richest stiff charts.) Uncle Marley made all that money by buying things very cheaply and then selling them for a lot of money. The grown-up way of describing this particular activity is 'import and export'. It's actually quite an easy way to make yourself very rich very quickly. (You might like to try this yourself by taking your dad's iPod into school (be sure to leave him a couple of pence in his loose change drawer so he can't accuse you of stealing) and selling it to a schoolmate for 20p. That's already a clear 18p profit with practically no effort on your part.)

The problem with rich people is that they don't get rich by being generous. This is why the richer Uncle Marley became the meaner he became. In the end he was so scared that he might have to give someone some of his money that he locked himself away in a great big house in the country and refused to come out until he was dead.

Felicity MacKenzie

Now for Felicity MacKenzie – Boo! Hiss! – sister of Uncle Marley and mother of Johnny Nothing. That's a picture of her above on her wedding day. Now how would you describe her? Well, physically she was the tallest and fattest person in the room. But this doesn't really give a true picture of her at all. She was one of those grown-ups who refuse to recognise that they are grown-ups.

By this I mean that although she exactly resembled a **DISGUSTINGLY** obese middle-aged woman at a funeral, she wore the clothing of a lithe young teenager at a school disco. She was dressed in a white T-shirt and sky blue jeans that might have looked rather fetching had she been thirty years younger, sixty pounds lighter and a completely different person altogether.

She looked like she been to the garage to put air in her car's tyres, and while bending over to tie her shoelaces somebody had put the air hose up her bum hole and switched it on to earn

£250 on 'You've Been Framed'. She looked like the Incredible Hulk just as he was getting angry and his clothes were starting to split. Except her body wasn't green. It was pink and floppy with stretch marks. Whenever she moved loose, wrinkly bits of it poked out in all sorts of places.

Most people who saw her immediately turned their eyes away out of sheer embarrassment. Those who did look at her usually looked away pretty quickly after being subjected to a mouthful of abuse that sounded something like this:

'What you lookin' at, you nosey bugger? Come over here and I'll give you a five-finger sandwich!' Whatever a five-finger sandwich is.

Although she was poor and born with an unfortunate allergy to work, Felicity MacKenzie always carried a cigarette between her teeth (and one behind her ear, ready for when the one between her teeth ran out of smoke (don't smoke kids!)). This was funded by Johnny's Child Support Allowance or by confiscating any birthday or Christmas money that had been sent to her son (which didn't happen very often, it has to be said).

Most people who know Felicity will agree that there's no easy way of describing what a truly horrible, nauseous, vile person she was. They say that at a certain age you get the face you deserve. Well she certainly deserved hers, which was milk-curdlingly ugly and home to the largest mouth in the South of England. Here's another example of her using it:

'Oi! You! Yes, you!,' (that's her talking to Mr. Dark, as she stands close to the body of her dead brother, smoking a cigarette and casually flicking ash into his open mouth). When you gonna read the will? Ain't got all bloody day you know!'

'Well… We have… We have… We have to… Finish the funeral first.'

I thought I'd kill two birds with one stone by also giving you an example of how Mr. Dark speaks. He's got a surprisingly posh accent, actually. And I didn't realise that he stuttered when he was flustered. But then a lot of people stutter when they're talking to Felicity Mackenzie.

Johnny Nothing

Finally, here's the most important character of all. Why, it's Johnny Nothing, of course. And since you've been so patient with me I'll put you out of your misery and tell you why he's so special. The clue is in the name. His mum's surname is MacKenzie but his is Nothing. Do you want to know why? I'll tell you.

What makes Johnny really special isn't the fact that during a school science class he was bitten by a radioactive spider and suddenly started squirting sticky spider juice out of his wrists and climbing up walls and getting all tingly at the first sign of trouble. He isn't from the planet Krypton and able to fly through the air or snap telegraph poles in two or use his x-ray vision to see what's underneath peoples' clothing. He didn't come third in the X-Factor and get a record deal. He didn't win a silver medal in the Paralympics. It wasn't any of these things.

What made Johnny different from everyone else in the school was the fact that he had nothing. That's right. Nothing.

Quite simply, Johnny was the poorest boy in the school. He had no toys. His clothes were all nicked from those bags that people leave outside charity shops. His shoes were his dad's hand-me-downs. (Or should I say 'foot-me-downs'?) That's right. Johnny wore his dad's old shoes. And since his dad was size 12 and Johnny was size 6 this meant that going for a walk in the park was certainly no walk in the park. Johnny never had any pocket money. In Johnny's house there wasn't a TV in sight. There was no toilet paper. And there was no newspaper to use as toilet paper (how did he wipe his bum? I hear you ask. Let's just say that people who lived in Johnny's house let their fingers do the wiping).

Johnny had nothing. Nothing at all. Less than nothing. Nothing times a million. Nothing minus ten. Nothing. Rein. Pas de tout. Zilch. www.nothing_at_all.com. Nothing. Not a bean.

Let's all give Johnny a group hug, shall we?

It was Johnny's blue meanie schoolmates that gave him the name 'Nothing'. It happened at the end of his very first day at school as he sat in the dinner hall nursing a packed lunch box on his lap that had no packed lunch in it. Some wise guy at the back called out 'Hey, look everyone... There's Johnny Nothing!' And everyone laughed and the name's kind of stuck ever since. It's even somehow entered the school computer system. So at registration each morning his teacher asks if Johnny Nothing is there. And even though the class erupts into raucous laughter every time he does this, he genuinely believes that it's Johnny's real name.

Hold on a minute. Let's hear Johnny say something shall we? Ready?

Back at the funeral Johnny was holding his mum's hand. Or rather, she was holding his hand. She'd been holding it very tightly for more than an hour now like it was a pound of sausages and it had gone numb. Johnny couldn't feel his fingers. He decided to ask if she'd mind letting go.

'Mum…' he said.

'Shhhhhhhhhhh!' said Mrs. MacKenzie.

'Mu…' he said.

'**SILENCE**!' growled Mrs. MacKenzie.

'M…'

'**SHUT UP BOY**!!' yelled Mrs. MacKenzie.

OK. So that's not a very good example of Johnny speaking. Don't worry, though. You'll get to hear him say a lot more before this book is over.

Chapter 03 – Kiss

There. That's all the main characters in the book dealt with. It's at this point that you might decide that you've had enough and go off and read something by Jacqueline Wilson or Roald Dahl instead. I wouldn't personally advise it. But there's no accounting for taste.

If, however, you've decided to tough it out for a while longer then it's your turn to do some work. You have some serious story reading to do. So come with me and imagine a big, dusty old church with Uncle Marley's icily cold body lying on its back at the front being stared at from the back by a handful of people who really didn't like it when it was icily warm. Phew.

Have you ever seen a dead body with all its insides scraped out (and maybe sold to the local kebab shop) and then stuffed to the brim with £50 notes? Neither have I. But from the expression on the faces of most of the people staring at Uncle Marley, this was exactly what they were seeing.

When they looked at Uncle Marley they just saw money. Rolls and rolls of banknotes. Bundles and bundles of bunce. Loads and loads of loot. Dollops and dollops of dough. A stash of cash. A wagonload of wonga. They saw a limitless supply of frozen horsemeat lasagne from Iceland. An everlasting collection of flat-packed cardboard boxes containing things that were impossible to put together from Argos. He was their cold, dead, smelly ticket to everything they had ever dreamed of.

If I had the time and I was feeling in the mood I could give you a lovely description of the interior of the church. You'd be really impressed. I could talk about how the warm summer sunshine was streaming in through the beautiful stained glass windows. About the exquisite carved wooden pulpit that dated back to Queen Victoria. About how John McVicar was secretly questioning the existence of God. Or about how the bloke playing the organ was growing really irritated because he was hardly getting a mention in this story.

But that would be rude because Ebenezer Dark was currently speaking:

'...so I think we're all agreed that Jake Marley was a very,very nice chap indeed... Lovely fellow... Splendid chap... Now for the reading of the will...'

In reality, of course, he said a lot more than this. But one of the good things about writing stories is that you can leave out whatever you feel like leaving out. And I'm leaving out most of what he said about Uncle Marley because it was pretty dull and I'm keen to get on with the action.

'About time, too!' said Mrs. MacKenzie grumpily agreeing with me. 'This is pretty dull and I'm keen to get on with the action!'

'As you all know, Mr. Marley was an extremely wealthy man...

He was also a very unconventional man... Mr. Marley liked to do things a little differently than most people...'

Everybody there silently agreed that Uncle Marley was indeed stinking rich. Rich and stinking. But nobody there was that aware that he liked to do things a little differently because when he was alive he never left his house. But that didn't stop Mr. Dark from reaching up and pulling back a huge curtain that he was standing in front of to reveal a giant flat screen TV. (Did I mention before that Mr. Dark was standing in front of a huge curtain that concealed a giant flat screen TV? Sorry if I didn't.)

'Many of you will not be aware that before he died, Mr. Marley didn't write a will...' explained Mr. Dark.

There was silence for a few moments while everyone tried to get their heads around the double negative in the last sentence. This was followed by a collective gasp of disappointment. Sort of: 'Haaawwwwwww!!' The sort of noise that people make when their favourite football team misses a penalty. One or two people said some pretty nasty swear words.

COMPETITION TIME

Because I'm not allowed to print them, I've left blank spaces to represent the swear words that were said.

1. 'You stupid *******!!!'
2. 'You stinking ***!!!'
3. 'Go to ******* ****!!!'

Feel free to fill in what you think was said and then send your answers to the following address to win a prize:

The Prime Minister,
10 Downing Street, London SW1A 2AA

Back to Mr. Dark:

'…instead, he recorded a short video that outlines exactly what he intended to do with his vast fortune.'

There was a collective gasp of relief from the gathering, sort of 'Yeeesssshhhhh!'. The sort of noise that people make at football matches when the opposition have just missed a penalty. One or two people reluctantly apologised for swearing.

'However, before I can play the video to you, I have a minor request.'

Mr. Dark self-consciously shuffled the papers he was holding and cleared his throat, making a noise that is almost impossible to describe in words. Sort of: 'Hhhmmppphh… Bedrummp-phh…'

No, that wasn't it.

'Mr. Marley was always touched by how much affection you had for him…' he intoned. 'And before he died, your love for him was an undoubted source of comfort…'

Some of the mourners raised their eyebrows. The rest simply lowered their eyeballs. Most people there hated Uncle Marley more than Brussels sprouts boiled in liquid horse manure served with rat tails on toast and knew that he hated them just as much. They were jealous of him: jealous of his wallet, jealous of his big house in the country, jealous of his giant TVs. They hated him as much as Itchy hated Scratchy. As much as grown-ups hate traffic wardens. As much as you hate homework (although there's always one or two sneaks who pretend to like homework. (If your teacher is reading this story to you right now, turn around and pull faces at the class sneaks to make them feel really uncomfortable.))

'…so before we play his video he thought it would be nice if you all gave him a tender kiss.'

There was silence in the church for a few moments as this comment sank in. And then Felicity MacKenzie's voice rang out: 'This is a joke, right? I'm not kissing a dead body – no matter who it is.'

'Quite right,' agreed her husband nervously.

'Not likely,' added Uncle Sydney.

Mr. Dark looked uncomfortable for a few seconds. Then his face hardened and he stared intently at the piece of paper he was holding before he spoke again. 'I'm sorry but I really must insist. It specifically says here that there will be no will unless everyone kisses Mr. Marley.'

'Why don't you kiss him then?' demanded Mrs. MacKenzie.

Once again Mr. Dark looked at the piece of paper. 'It says here that I mustn't kiss Mr. Marley. Which is a great pity, you know, because I was terribly fond of him.'

'Gimme that piece of paper!' ordered Mrs. Mackenzie.

Mr. Dark looked a little scared for a moment and hugged the paper to his chest. His face softened then it hardened again. Then it finally softened one last time: 'It says here that if anyone else reads this paper the will is cancelled,' he said cagily.

The gathering once more fell silent for a moment and then Billy MacKenzie spoke for the second time in this story. 'Come on Fliss', he said ('Fliss' was what Billy sometimes called Felicity. Like a lot of people he was simply too lazy to be bothered to pronounce all the syllables in a name. It was too much like hard work.). 'Just get it over with. Think of the dosh.'

There was a further spell of silence as everyone wondered what they were going to do next. It was bad enough spending a morning sniffing a dead man but kissing him?

'Oh very well!' said Mrs. MacKenzie angrily, looking over at Mr. Dark and then at her husband. 'Go ahead and kiss him then.'

'Me? Why should I?' said Mr. MacKenzie looking aghast.

'You do it then!' ordered Mrs. MacKenzie, turning towards Sydney.

'After you,' replied her brother, edging away from the coffin.

Mrs. MacKenzie stood and looked at the body of her brother for a few moments. She turned her nose up at the smell, which seemed to be getting worse with every second. She crinkled up her nostrils. She shrugged her shoulders. She closed her eyes. She bravely clenched her large and floppy bottom cheeks. Then, without warning, she reached over and very quickly planted the briefest of kisses on one of Uncle Marley's cheeks. A bit like the one that you give to your grandma when she tries to kiss you with a runny wet mouth that tastes of old humbugs.

'Ugggggghhhh!' she spluttered, showering Mr. Dark with a delicate fountain of spittle. 'Happy now?'

Ebenezer Dark slowly shook his head and once more regarded the paper he was holding. 'I'm sorry but that won't do,' he said, although from the tone of his voice he didn't really seem that sorry at all. 'It's says here that you have to kiss Mr. Marley on the lips.'

'You what?!' exclaimed Mrs. MacKenzie. 'I'm not kissing a dead man on the lips!'

Mr. Dark shrugged his shoulders. 'Then there's no will,' he said. 'It's all written down here in black and white.'

'Really!' said Mrs. MacKenzie. 'This is outrageous!' Nevertheless, after a moment of hesitation she reached over to the corpse of her brother and quickly gave him another kiss, this time on the lips.

'Your turn,' she said in relief, spitting something gunky onto the floor and looking angrily towards her husband.

'I'm terribly sorry,' interrupted Mr. Dark. 'But it says here that the kiss must be for at least half a minute or all of Mr. Marley's money will go to Battersea Dogs Home or somewhere else like that.'

Mrs. MacKenzie looked like she was going to explode. Her face turned bright crimson until it began to resemble one of those tomato-shaped ketchup dispensers full of vinegary red fluid that you get in poor peoples' cafés. She did a lot of cursing under her breath then she yelled: 'I'm not doing that you horrible little creep!'

'Very well,' replied Mr. Dark, starting to put away his papers.

Mrs. MacKenzie took a deep breath and swore again. 'This is the last time,' she scowled.

Almost in slow motion, Mrs. MacKenzie moved her face closer to her dead brother's. She took a nose-full of the horrible foetid smell that was pumping from the corpse and closed her eyes tightly. Then she pressed her mouth to Uncle Marley's cold, blue lips and waited.

Standing in front of the curtain Mr. Dark looked at his watch and began to count.

After only ten seconds Mrs. MacKenzie began to feel faint. She could feel her dead brother's whiskers tickling her chin and she could taste his dead taste. (Strangely enough, he tasted like Southern Fried Chicken.)

After twenty seconds her stomach was making strange gurgling noises like a dishwasher stuck in rinse mode. In her mouth the taste of Uncle Marley flavour Southern Fried Chicken was replaced by sausage, bacon, egg and beans with brown sauce and egg yolk all mixed up in the beans. This was what she had had for breakfast that morning.

After thirty seconds what remained of that breakfast was

splashed over her shoes in quite a nice pattern as it happens. You could easily have framed it and hung it in the Tate Modern. And she emerged, breathless, white and gasping for air from what had been the longest kiss of her life and – coincidentally – the longest kiss of Uncle Marley's death.

'Will that do?' she garbled weakly, hardly able to speak as she moved away from the corpse on unsteady legs.

'Yes, I believe so,' said Mr. Dark, smiling politely.

'Now it's your turn,' she coughed. Staring over at the horrified faces of the other two men.

'No need,' said Mr. Dark jauntily, looking once again at the piece of paper. 'It says here that if anyone here brings up their breakfast while kissing Mr. Marley the others are excused from doing it. It's only fair and decent.'

Chapter 04 – Will

The giant flat screen TV suddenly flickered into life and the face of Uncle Marley squinted out into the church. He looked quite a bit healthier than the other Uncle Marley, who was still resting in his wooden box waiting to feed the worms. This one was fairly clean-shaven and less dead looking. Occasionally he could be seen to gulp in a huge mouthful of air, something the other Uncle Marley hadn't attempted for quite some time.

'Oh, there you are,' said the once alive Uncle Marley squinting into the darkness. 'Thought I'd see the usual suspects here. Come for my money have you?'

The small gathering of mourners stared towards the screen with a mixture of disbelief, hatred and impatience – I think the word is 'dishatience' – as Uncle Marley continued.

'You there Felicity?' he called out. 'Don't know why I'm bothering to ask because there's no way that your fat, ugly mush would keep away if there's money in it for you.'

Mrs. MacKenzie, who had regained a little of her composure by now, let out a hoot of outrage and began to yell at her ex-brother. I did actually write down what she said but this book's spoilsport editor removed her words; apparently you could get arrested just for reading them.

'He can't hear you, you know,' said Uncle Sydney dryly.

'That idiot-brained husband of yours there, too?' asked the figure on the screen. 'Bet he can't keep away. I'll expect he'll be wanting to waste his share on booze and women.'

Billy MacKenzie reddened a little and stared guiltily at his feet. His feet stared back as if to say: 'What are you looking at, chum?' His wife glowered at him.

'You there as well Sydney? What a loser! I suppose you're going to spend your share on fags and horses are you?'

Johnny Nothing was watching all of this with interest. The boring funeral had suddenly perked up a little. He had never met Uncle Marley before and certainly hadn't ever heard him speak. He was beginning to understand why his parents didn't like Jake Marley very much. Uncle Marley didn't mince his words (if he did, they'd probably come out in little gnarled up chunks and you could make wordburgers and chips or Spaghetti with wordballs from them). Johnny wondered when it would be his turn to be humiliated but for the time being Uncle Marley seemed unaware that he was there.

'Right then, small-talk over,' the figure continued, 'Let's get down to the nitty gritty, shall we?

'A couple of months ago my doctor told me that I was dying of cancer. Didn't bother me at the time. After all, I've had a fortunate life. My business has given me more money than I could ever have dreamed about. I've eaten good food, gone to some pretty phenomenal places and been out with more than my fair share of beautiful women…

'Yes, I've had a good time – a far better time than all you useless wasters. And you know why? Because I'm cleverer than you are.

'So this is the deal: I've got more than £40 million in my bank account and I can either flush it down the toilet or I can give it to somebody. And even though I haven't seen any of you in years and can't say that I've wanted to, I guess the fact that we're blood relatives should mean something…

Uncle Marley looked downwards and picked up a notebook. 'Got a list here somewhere… Here it is… Right – let me put you all out of your misery and then you can all bugger off home…'

Uncle Marley paused for a few moments, as if trying to build up the tension. It worked. 'First of all let's deal with Sydney,' he announced. 'Ebenezer? Are you there? Can you do the honours?'

The figure on the video stared in the direction of Mr. Dark. Almost as if he knew where the other man was standing. 'Yes sir,' said Mr. Dark, moving briskly towards Uncle Sydney with a small white envelope in his hand.

'I'm not giving you any money,' said Uncle Marley. 'Instead I'm giving you something that will be much more use to you. In this envelope is a token that will entitle you to a lifetime's supply of cigarettes. Just take it into any newsagents or tobacconists day or night and they'll give you as many cigarettes as you like.'

Uncle Sydney took the envelope and tore it open. From the expression on his face it was difficult to work out if he was disappointed or pleased.

'Since you've spent most of your life trying to smoke yourself to death I thought I'd give you a hand,' continued Uncle Marley (don't smoke kids!). 'It also make sound business sense to me because the more cigarettes you smoke the less you'll need… I'm sure even you can work it out if you think about it.'

The other adults in the room looked more than a little shocked. They had all spent the weeks leading up to the funeral working themselves into a soapy lather about how they were going to spend Uncle Marley's money. Things had suddenly taken a turn for the worse.

'Billy, now it's your turn,' said the figure on the video with a sigh. 'Lazy Billy. Never done a day's work in your life…"

Once more Uncle Marley looked over in the direction of his assistant. 'Ebenezer,' he said.

Mr. Dark stepped forward clutching a large cardboard box in his hands. It appeared very heavy. The solicitor could hardly hold it. He passed it over to Billy MacKenzie, who ripped the box open eagerly. Inside was a set of weights and some exercise gear.

Uncle Marley was struggling to hold back a smile as he spoke: 'I didn't want to encourage your bad ways so no money for you either. I've left you something that will help you get rid of that big fat grotesque beer belly of yours.'

Billy MacKenzie's face went pale and his jaw dropped to the floor in disappointment. After a moment or so he picked it up and garbled a few words under his breath. Then he gave Uncle Marley's gift a vicious kick and let out a yelp of pain. The others looked on aghast as he hopped around the floor of the church clutching his injured toe.

'Now for the lovely, delightful Felicity,' said Uncle Marley, obviously oblivious to Billy's pain. 'I've got a special present for you.'

Felicity MacKenzie scowled. She was already suspecting the worst. She nervously pointed her red, tomatoey face towards the screen.

'What happened to that pretty little girl that I used to know all those years ago?' said Uncle Marley wistfully. 'How did you become that big ugly evil monster that you are now? Who knows what happened to change you? But I'm here to help… Ebenezer.'

Mr. Dark moved towards Mrs. MacKenzie clutching an ever bigger box than the one he had given to her husband. He placed it at the feet of the woman, who stood and looked it at in disdain. She was in no hurry to open it.

'Open it,' urged Uncle Marley.

'Yes, open it,' said Uncle Sydney, dolefully clutching his cigarette token.

The box was made of stiff white cardboard and secured at the top with a red ribbon. Mrs. MacKenzie waited for a few moments, as if afraid to see what was inside and then gingerly pulled at the ribbon. The box fell open to reveal… Nothing. It was completely empty.

'What's the meaning of this!' yelled Mrs. MacKenzie edging towards the screen angrily.

'Thought you'd like it,' smiled Uncle Marley. 'Of all the people I know you're the person who would benefit the most from a little fresh air. And this box is full of it.'

Mrs. MacKenzie let out a blood curdling scream and finally released her grip on Johnny's hand. Johnny had never seen his mother look so angry. Her head seem to inflate like a balloon, her eyes bulged until they were about to pop. From her mouth came a battery of swear words and expletives that made the vicar and the organist turn their faces to the floor and frantically start crossing themselves.

There was a tearing noise as the dress she was wearing began to split under the strain of it all. Billy MacKenzie cowered away from his wife in abject terror. He had eaten a very large, very hot, positively volcanic curry the night before. Throughout the morning he had been concentrating very hard on trying to keep its residual odours inside his trousers.

Normally Billy wouldn't have been too concerned about letting rip in front of other people but he recognised that this was supposed to be a solemn occasion and that the pungent aroma of delicate Indian herbs and spices mixed together with crude, untreated methane gas might not be that appropriate.

However, his wife's screeches and yowls were too much to bear and the tension finally overcame Mr. MacKenzie. He closed his eyes and produced a long overdue trouser explosion that by an eerie coincidence sounded uncannily like the creaking of Uncle Marley's coffin. All eyes turned towards his corpse, almost expecting it to rise from its box and shout 'April Fool!'.

Surprised and pleased that nobody had noticed his gas leak, Billy crinkled up his flabby face and sniffed the air in disgust. 'My God that body stinks,' he said.

John McVicar eyed him suspiciously.

Chapter 05 – Task

You know on TV when the Queen accidentally drops her crown on her big toe and then loses her temper and smacks Prince Philip round the head with her sceptre? Or a bit of cucumber sandwich goes down the front of her dress which was clean on only that morning and she kicks one of her Corgis up the tail-end in frustration? Have you ever noticed that they tend to replace what she says in this type of situation with a beeping noise? It sounds like this: 'beep!' And sometimes like this: 'beep!' Well I'm going to have to do that now in order to make what Mrs. MacKenzie said in the church a little more printable.

What she said was: 'You beeeep beeeeep!! You can stuff your money up your beep-beep. You stingy old beeep!! So go and beep yourself and beep-beep-beep-beeeeeeeeeeeep!!!'

And a lot more besides.

This sort of went on for some time until she gradually began to run out of swear words. If she'd had a thesaurus in her handbag she would probably have fished it out and tried to find a few more. But as it was she had to make do with what she'd got. Gradually, however, as the others looked on, her face began to regain some of its usual colouring and she stopped looking quite so much like a tomato dispenser. Her breathing became a little more regular. Finally, she turned angrily towards the image on the screen of her smiling brother, who seemed to be waiting patiently for her to speak.

'I shan't pretend I'm surprised by this,' she announced. 'You always were a rotten, mean, miserable, rancid old beep beep beep!!'

And a lot more besides.

She looked around her. At Uncle Sydney, who seemed bemused by the gift he had received. At her husband, Billy, who was still rubbing his injured toe and looking miserable. At Mr. Dark, who was obviously trying as hard as he could to not laugh. And at Johnny, who stood cowering a few feet away from her, worrying about what his mother was going to do next.

What she did do next was this: without saying a word she marched over to the coffin. She stood upright and looked at the body of her brother in silence for a few moments. Then she raised her hand and with all the energy she could muster gave his face a solid slap. The noise of the blow reverberated around the church. It was quite a pleasant sound actually. You should try it.

'Mrs. MacKenzie, how could you!' said John McVicar reproachfully. He was not really used to people whacking his dead bodies and secretly wondered if he should be charging a small fee.

'That'll teach you,' she mumbled angrily under her breath.

And with that Mrs. MacKenzie once more took hold of Johnny's hand. With her other she grabbed her husband by the nape of his neck like a cat carrying off a kitten. 'Goodbye,' she said to no-one in particular. 'And may he rot in hell.'

The trio had just reached the church door and were about to exit when the voice of Uncle Marley rang out once more. 'Thought you'd be pleased with that,' he said. 'Now be off with you and let me get on with being dead. I've got a lot of dead people to insult… Oh… Before I forget… I have one more gift… You there Johnny?'

Johnny heard his name being mentioned and halted in his tracks. He tried to stop his mother from pulling him outside the church. 'Mum! Stop!' he urged.

It was really very out of character for Johnny, who was scared stiff of his mother. He usually did everything she asked without question. He realised. However, that if he left the church there would be a very good chance that this book would be over right here and now. Nobody really wants that. Do they?

'Ignore him, Johnny,' ordered Mrs. MacKenzie. 'I've had enough of his stupid games!'

Uncle Marley's voice continued: 'You didn't think I'd leave you out did you, Johnny? You're the only one among that rotten lot who's worth anything at all…"

'Mum!' Johnny cried out again.

'SILENCE!' commanded his mother in capital letters. 'We're leaving!'

But Johnny was desperate to see his gift. Even if was a joke gift like everybody else's, it was still a gift. And it had been a long, long time since anyone had bought Johnny a gift.

With monumental effort Johnny managed to pull his hand out from his mother's vice-like grip. People say 'vice-like grip' a lot don't they? Let's change that last sentence to: With monumental effort Johnny managed to pull his hand out from his mother's really very tight indeed grip. Actually, I think 'vice-like grip' sounds better after all. Let's stick with that.

'Ebenezer, could you please give Johnny his… His… Package…' said Uncle Marley.

'Stop right there!' shouted Johnny's mother as her son scampered to the front of the church like Roadrunner being chased by Wile E. Coyote, where Mr. Dark was holding a small briefcase.

'Open it, Johnny,' urged Uncle Marley.

Johnny took the case from Mr. Dark and held it in his hands. It felt empty but when he gently shook it he could hear something rattling around inside.

As he looked at the briefcase he was joined by his parents. Mrs. MacKenzie was even more angry than ever. 'How dare you disobey me, you little runt!' she breathlessly cried.

Johnny ignored his mother and opened the briefcase and felt around. There were three things inside: an envelope, a mobile phone with charger and a small address book.

'Open the envelope first,' instructed the voice on the screen.

Johnny did as he was told and was surprised to find that it contained a small plastic card. Attached to it was a yellow Post-It note with a four-digit number written on it.

Uncle Marley cleared his throat: 'I doubt that you've ever seen one of these before…'

'I have,' said Johnny, 'it's a cash card.'

'…it's called a cash card,' Uncle Marley continued. 'On that piece of paper is a number. If you put that card into any cash point and input the number, you will find that there is £1 million available in a bank account for you to spend.'

There was a stunned silence in the church. The only noise that could be heard was the sound of John McVicar dropping a small pin on the floor that he had just found in the one of his jacket pockets.

Johnny looked at the card. Then he looked at the screen. Uncle Marley was smiling. 'That's £1 million for you to do with what you like,' he said.

Johnny looked at his mother. Then his father. Then uncle Sydney. Everybody looked dazed. Nobody said a word.

'I'm giving you an opportunity in life, Johnny,' continued Uncle Marley. 'I know all about you. I know all about the way that that sister of mine treats you. Sometimes we all need a break in life. But the opportunity comes with a condition."

'Hmmmpphhh! I thought it was too good to be true!' exclaimed Mrs. MacKenzie.

'It would be too easy for you to go out and spend that money straight away. Get a new bike… Or a PlayStation… Or some decent clothes. And Lord knows I wouldn't blame you in the least. But I've got a task for you, Johnny. Are you listening?'

Johnny nodded.

'Your task is to come back to this church in exactly one year's time and I want you to have more than £1 million in that bank account. It doesn't matter if it's only a penny more than the original sum. I want you to come back here in profit. Because life's all about profit. If you can manage to do that I will give you ten times what you have. Can you imagine that Johnny? You will have £10 million put into that bank account! This will set you and your children up for life. Mr. Dark over there will see to it.

'As tasks go it's a lot easier than you might think. You're going to learn that once you have money it not difficult at all to turn that money into even more money. You could, for example, put all that money on a winning horse. That wouldn't be too difficult, would it?"

Once again, Johnny nodded.

'Or you could try your hand at the stock market. That's an easy way to win – and lose – a fortune. But far simpler would be to just keep it in the bank and not touch it at all. If you do this the bank will pay you interest on the money. You'll get… Let's see… more than £100 per day… Perhaps £200… Plenty enough to keep you in computer games and sweets or whatever it is that boys of your age are into.

'Remember: all you have to do is is come back here in a year's time with just a penny more than the original £1 million and you'll have completed your task.'

Now Johnny looked over at his mother. She stood as still and as silent but not quite as attractive as one of the stone gargoyles outside the church.

Uncle Marley cleared his throat one more time:

'Before we say farewell, one more thing. You'll notice that there is also a mobile phone in that case. Programmed into that mobile phone is just one number: Mr. Dark's over there."

Mr. Dark gave a self-conscious wave.

'I've left instructions for Ebenezer to give you assistance should you ever need it. You can call him at any time – night or day – if you need any advice or even if you just want someone to talk to.

'Also in the case is an address book. This has got the name

and details of your bank manager as well as Ebenezer's address. You never know when you might need to speak to him. I think that's everything. All that remains is for me to wish you good luck and a prosperous year. Hopefully, I'll be seeing you back here in exactly 365 days time. Off you go now.'

And with that Uncle Marley gave a brief smile, an even briefer wink, a short thumbs up and then the screen went black.

Johnny put the three objects back into the briefcase and felt his mother's fingers grasp hold of his hand even tighter than before. 'Come on darling…' she said, leading him out of the church. Johnny was a little taken aback because he had never heard his mother call him 'darling'. 'Time to go home and have a nice cup of tea.'

He'd never heard her say that either.

Johnny and his parents exited the church into the bright summer sunshine. As they did so Mrs. MacKenzie lowered her face to his and did something that she very rarely if ever did – she kissed Johnny on the cheek. He was more than a little shocked and he could smell the faint odour of Southern Fried Chicken.

Then, in one smooth motion, Mrs. MacKenzie reached over and snatched the briefcase from Johnny's grasp. 'You'd better give this to me,' she said. 'For safe-keeping.'

Chapter 06 – Money #1

Parents – I'm sure you'll agree – are very different to you. They sprout hair in **RIDICULOUS** places. They shed hair in others. They have bizarre, flabby, bobbly bits that wobble about in slow motion when they run. They leave absolutely **HORRENDOUS**, unspeakable stinks in the bathroom that make you **GAG**.

They cover the sink with bristles. They own hundreds of bottles of weird coloured liquids that they drink or swallow or inhale or stick up their bottoms. They smother their faces in gloopy cream that they think makes them look younger but in fact makes them look exactly the same age as before only smothered in gloopy cream. They definitely come from another planet – a pretty rancid one at that.

They are also contrary creatures. They say one thing and do

another.

They put you to bed early but stay up late. They forbid you to eat sweets and then fill their fat, greasy faces with chocolate as soon as you're not looking. They order you not to swear and then curse at the TV when Simon Cowell comes on. They demand you are careful with the pitiful amount of pocket money that they give you and then pack the house with stupid electronic gadgets or handbags or shoes that cost a disgusting amount of money.

In other words, a parent who actually follows their own advice is about as rare as a PE teacher who doesn't have a pot belly.

Johnny Nothing's parents were constantly warning him not to waste money. 'Look after your pennies,' Mrs. MacKenzie was fond of saying, 'and they'll grow into pounds.' Which is a little strange because Johnny never had any pennies, even on his birthday or at Christmas. And even stranger because now that Mrs. MacKenzie was holding on to her son's briefcase 'for safe keeping' she was spending money like it had gone out of fashion, been given away to the local Oxfam and then come back into fashion and been bought back for twice the price she originally paid for it.

Between you and me, the first thing that Mrs. MacKenzie did as soon as she left the church was not to go home for a cup of tea as she promised. What she did instead was tear open Uncle Marley's briefcase and rip out the cash card. Then, after a bit of hunting around for the nearest cashpoint she proceeded to withdraw hundreds and hundreds of pounds. And I mean hundreds and hundreds. Loads and loads of money. She had difficulty finding enough pockets to put it in.

Waving away Johnny's protests as if she were swatting an irritating wasp that keeps landing on your trifle, she then flagged down a taxi like it was an hourly occurrence and said only one word to the driver: 'Harrods'.

If you've never been to Harrods let me give you a brief description: It's a really big department store in West London that sells just about anything you can think of and a lot of other things you can't. It's a place where the poshest and richest people in the world go to spend their money and get charged three times the price that they would pay had they just popped out to the corner shop. It's also a place where poor people go to pretend that they are rich while they watch rich people become poorer.

Because it's so posh, the people at Harrods are a little choosy about who they allow in to spend their money. They have uniformed guards on the door – not to stop robbers from getting out but to stop shoppers from getting in. If you're wearing ripped jeans then you can't come in. If you're carrying a backpack you can't come in. If you've eaten too much food you can't come in.

Which is why when the guard standing at the Harrods front entrance spotted the taxi containing the MacKenzie family pulling up he immediately pressed a small round button on his right lapel. The button activated a secret electronic signal that went up and down the building a couple of times until it eventually arrived at the basement. There a message flashed up on a computer screen which read: '**WARNING! POOR PEOPLE!**'. Sitting in front of the computer, a bored Harrods employee quickly contacted security staff: 'Looks like we may have an incident at the main entrance,' he said.

Mrs. MacKenzie hoisted herself out of the taxi and handed the driver a wedge of tenners as if she had just won the lottery (which, in her mind, she had). Then she grabbed hold of her husband and Johnny and prepared to enter the store.

'One moment, madam,' said the security guard in a polite but firm voice. 'I'm afraid you can't come in.'

Mrs. MacKenzie looked the guard up and down a few times in the way that a lion looks at a deer it is just about to eat. He self-consciously took a step backwards.

'Why not?' she asked calmly.

'Because you can't.'

'Is my money not as good as anybody else's, you cheeky bugger?'

'It's not that, madam,' the guard announced smugly. 'It's just that the boy looks like he's stepped out of the pages of 'Oliver!'. And your husband looks like he's won first prize in The Worst Dressed Vagrant Of The Year Award.'

Mrs. MacKenzie's face turned cadmium red; a little bit of steam could be seen coming out of her ears.

'And no disrespect but[5] I don't think Harrods is your sort of place.'

Mrs. MacKenzie smiled. And then she frowned. Then the frown turned into a scowl. Then the scowl turned into a look of pure murder. Then the look of pure murder surprisingly turned back into a smile. Well, it was more of a grimace actually. A bit like this:

(:–/)

She reached into a pocket and pulled out a fistful of banknotes.

'Is it the sort of place that accepts these?' she asked, handing the wad of paper to the guard.

---

5 If anyone ever starts a sentence with 'no disrespect but...' this generally means that they are about to say the most disrespectful thing imaginable.

The guard looked around nervously to see if anyone was looking and then snatched the money and quickly stuffed it into his jacket pocket. 'Awfully sorry, madam,' he said, bowing as if the Queen had suddenly turned up and then beckoning them inside eagerly. 'My mistake. Please have a wonderful time shopping.'

And with that he stepped aside and let the scruffy looking trio enter. He watched as they headed for the lifts and then he pressed another button, this time on his left lapel. Down in the basement another message flashed up on the computer screen: '**FALSE ALARM**,' it read, '**RICH PERSON ENTERING**'.

The MacKenzie family were already learning that money can get you into any place that you want. Mrs. MacKenzie clutched the cash card in her hand as the three of them pushed through the crowds of shoppers. 'Mum... Are you sure that we should be doing this?' asked Johnny nervously, remembering the task that Uncle Marley had set him only an hour or so earlier.

His mother smiled at him. Except it wasn't a smile. It was a look of pain mixed with frustration and anger and bile. It was the sort of face that people pull when the chocolate drop they thought they were eating turns out to be a little pellet of rabbit poo.

'It won't matter if we spend a teensy-weensy bit,' explained Mrs. MacKenzie, scarcely able to hide her irritation. 'Didn't you hear your Uncle Marley? We'll earn this all back in interest before you know it."

As his mother marched away purposefully, Johnny couldn't help noticing that she was tenderly stroking the cash card like most people would stroke a pet hamster.

Chapter 07 – Shopping

Here are some of the things that Mrs. MacKenzie bought at Harrods:

FUR COAT	£2,600
a NEW SUIT FOR BILLY MacKENZIE	£449
a 56-INCH FLAT SCREEN 3D TV	£3,500
SOME SHOES	£220
SOME MORE SHOES	£360
EVEN MORE SHOES	£280
a DISHWASHER	£900
a CRATE OF WINE	£240
a HANDBAG	£299
ANOTHER HANDBAG	£199
a HARRODS FOOD HAMPER	£450
AN iPOD TOUCH	£320
an iPaD	£598
SOME SHOES	£320
TOTAL	£10,735

Chapter 08 – Boxes

'Has she won the lottery?' asked one of the neighbours.

'Maybe she's mugged someone,' announced another.

'Perhaps' she's mugged a lottery winner,' said yet another.

Johnny Nothing and his parents lived in a small two-bedroom flat on the eighth floor of a tower block at the centre of a very unpleasant council estate. It was the sort of place where on a good day the lifts were filled with a pungent home-brew of doggy wee wee and human wee wee. Almost as if a Staffordshire Bull Terrier and its owner had been caught short at exactly the same time and couldn't be bothered to wait for the lift to get to its floor. On a bad day the delightful odours of this piquant cocktail were often masked by the aroma of something a little more solid, which steamed when the weather was cold.

The building had been standing largely neglected for a very,

very long time. In fact, the local council had more or less forgotten all about it. If it was a man it would be one of those old tramps that you see in the town centre yelling swear words at some invisible person.

The walls of the tower block were covered in graffiti, evidently written by people who had not yet learned how to spell. Instead of flowers, the gardens of the council estate were decorated with long discarded KFC boxes, televisions with smashed up screens, rusting bits of car exhaust pipe, discarded used sticking plasters, the odd dead cat and assorted bits of anonymous rubbish. The occupants of the estate were apparently so poor that they could not afford dustbins, choosing instead to throw their waste from the balconies of the building on to the ever-growing but never-collected heap of trash.

All sorts of people of different races, colours and creeds had the unhappy privilege of living on the estate. And they all had one thing in common: money. Or rather a lack of it. Which is why Felicity MacKenzie and her sudden spending spree did not escape her neighbours' attentions. Soon she was the talk of the estate.

***

On the morning after the funeral and the afternoon spent at Harrods the MacKenzie family had a bit of a lie-in. This was not completely unexpected as Mr. and Mrs. MacKenzie had been up partying until the very early hours and had kept Johnny awake.

They had celebrated their good fortune by ringing up the local take-away pizza place and ordering everybody on the estate a pizza. When you consider that there were almost a thousand people living on the estate and the average price of pizza was

£5 you can work out for yourself how much this cost. Strangely enough the only person who didn't get a pizza was Johnny. He made himself some toast.

It was Johnny who woke up first that morning, dragging himself out of the tiny bed in his tiny bedroom and pushing past all the gift boxes and empty wine bottles and crisp packets that lined the staircase. Indeed, there were so many cardboard boxes in the flat that it was almost impossible to move.

Johnny manoeuvred himself to the kitchen and made some cereal. Then he listened to the sound of his parents snoring. The sound resembled a horde of basking rhinos on an African savanna. After a while the noise ceased and he heard the sound of his parents descending the stairs, knocking over a few boxes as they did so.

First to arrive was Billy MacKenzie. 'Morning boy,' he said gruffly. Mr. MacKenzie very rarely called his son by his name. It was as if he couldn't remember the name of his only child. Next to arrive was his mum. 'Johnny, where's my coffee?' she whined as if she only had minutes to live. 'You know I need my coffee in the morning!'

As Johnny made his mother a cup of instant coffee there was only one thing on his mind. He wanted to know when he was going to get his cash card back. After seeing his mother hold on to his inheritance for 'safe keeping' for less than one day he wasn't sure that it was the safest place to keep his card.

Johnny had been doing a lot of thinking. He kept hearing the words of Uncle Marley on the big TV screen:

'Your task is to come back to this church in exactly one year's time and I want you to have more than £1 million in that bank account. If you can manage to do that I will give you ten times what you have. You will have £10 million put into that bank account.'

Johnny kept running that figure through his mind. £1 million was already more money than he could possibly imagine but ten times that figure was frankly unbelievable. He thought of all the things that they could do with £10 million. They could buy a Rolls Royce. Ten Rolls Royces. A castle. A hundred Playstations. A million packets of wine gums. Anything they wanted.

All he had to do was to somehow stop his mother from spending too much of the money. He knew that it wasn't going to be easy.

He waited until his mother had drunk three or four cups of coffee before he broached the subject. 'Mum,' he said gingerly, as she sat in the kitchen smoking a cigarette and eating a plate of cold pizza from last night. Her face was pale and her eyes were vacant as if in a trance.

'Hmmm?'

'I was wondering if…'

'Hmmm?'

'…I was wondering if you could let me have my thing back today.'

'Thing? What thing?'

'You know… The thing that Uncle Marley left me in his will… The cash card…'

Mrs. MacKenzie quickly snapped out of her trance and sat bolt upright as if she had sat on a drawing pin. She ran her eyes over her son and a very nasty expression spread over her face a bit like ink spreads on blotting paper. Johnny had seen that expression many times in the past. She usually used it when he had done something wrong. Or if Billy MacKenzie had done something wrong. Or if she just plain felt like picking on somebody.

But then the expression disappeared and was replaced by a kinder sort of look. Johnny had also seen that look many times in the past. His mother used it when she wanted something. Like when she was feeling lazy and wanted him to go to the off license and pick up some beer or cigarettes for her. Or when she was broke and wanted to get some food on credit from the corner shop.

He knew his mother well enough to recognise that there was an inner battle being waged inside her. He could tell that she wanted to scream and shout at him but was trying her hardest to hold back.

'Not yet, darling,' she said, using that word for the second time. If you could hear her speaking I can guarantee that you have never heard the word 'darling' spoken in such a mean, evil, vindictive way. 'Not yet, darling… You see, I'm a lot older than you and much more… What's the word now? Responsible, that's it. **RESPONSIBLE**. You're far too young to look after that that amount of money.'

'But Mum…'

'No buts, my lad, you'll get your card back when the time is right…'

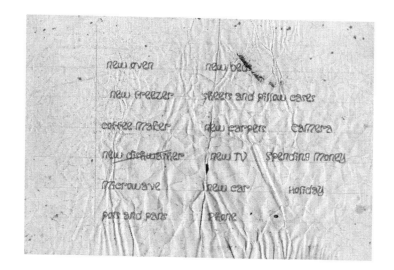

new oven   new beds

new freezer   sheets and pillow cases

coffee maker   new carpets   camera

new dishwasher   new TV   spending money

microwave   new car   holiday

pots and pans   phone

Chapter 09 – List

Later that same morning the MacKenzie family squeezed in among the boxes in their cramped living room and Felicity MacKenzie made an announcement. Her appearance was changing. She was dressed in some of the new clothes that she had bought yesterday. All of them had designer labels but none of them were quite large enough to accommodate her bulk. She had paid a small fortune for them but right now it looked like she was wearing something that had shrunk in the wash.

'I've decided that we need to do a little shopping today,' she said. 'Just one or two essentials, mind you.'

She held a piece of paper in one hand and a pen in the other. She began to write. 'Let's see,' she said. 'We'll need a few things for the flat…

'First of all a new oven…

'And a new freezer, of course…

'Then there's a new coffee maker…

'And a new dishwasher…'

'Mum.'

'And a microwave…

'Mum.'

'And some new pots and pans…'

'Mum.'

'What is it Johnny?'

'Well it's nothing… But… You bought a new dishwasher yesterday.'

'Did I? Oh… So I did… Never mind, I'll cross that one off the list.'

Mrs. MacKenzie thought for a moment before continuing:

'Then there's new beds for us, of course…

'And new sheets and pillow cases…

'And new carpets…

'What about a new TV?' piped up Billy MacKenzie.

'Good idea… A new TV…' said Mrs. MacKenzie, writing it down.

'But Mum, you got a new TV yesterday,' interrupted Johnny.

'Did I? Never mind – you can never have too many TVs. We'll put this one in our bedroom.'

Mrs. MacKenzie continued in this vein for several minutes until three pieces of paper were completely filled.

'I think that's it for now,' she said. 'Unless anyone else can think of anything.'

'Well I wouldn't mind a new car,' said Billy MacKenzie. 'And a little spending money. Oh… and one of those nice phones that have a camera and let's you play music.'

'Car… Money… Phone… Camera… Music…' Mrs. MacKenzie wrote it down.

'Oh and how about we have a party?' said Mr. MacKenzie.

'Party…'

'Oh… And while we're at it why don't we take a holiday?'

Mrs. MacKenzie wrote this down with a look of triumph on her face. 'I really feel that we've achieved something today,' she said. 'Now let's call a taxi and get to work.'

Chapter 10 – Holiday

ow that the MacKenzie family was rich the world was their lobster. 'I'm going on a trip!' announced Felicity MacKenzie a couple of days after her latest spending spree. 'And since it's school holidays Johnny can come too. Say thank-you, Johnny.'

'Thank-you,' said Johnny weakly.

So the family packed up their belongings: Mrs. MacKenzie took four large trunks full of clothing, make-up and baked beans (in case she didn't like foreign food). Mr. MacKenzie took two medium sized suitcases crammed with copies of the Racing Post, electronic gadgets and cans of lager (in case he didn't like foreign beer). Johnny took a Sainsbury's carrier bag stuffed with a few comics, some pencils and a change of underpants.

The trio boarded a plane to Paris in France. The grown-ups sat at the front in first class, sipping champagne and eating posh caviare sandwiches. Johnny sat at the back of the plane in economy class. There he read his comics and tried to ignore the chorus of howling babies that surrounded him. (Most airlines make it compulsory that there is at least one howling baby in the cheaper section of the plane. The idea is to encourage passengers to pay extra to go and sit in the expensive section of the plane. For long haul flights they try to ensure that there is at least three howling babies per passenger.)

When they got to Paris it took Mrs. MacKenzie only a day or so to get **BORED** with the French. She objected to the fact that most of them didn't speak English. And when her attempts at speaking French failed she grew restless. (In other words, she did what most English tourists do when they are abroad – she spoke English, only slower and louder than usual and expected everyone to understand what she was going on about.)

After copping an eyeful of the big tower in Paris she insisted that the family get on another plane and go somewhere better. Over the next couple of weeks they flew all over the world at tremendous cost. But nowhere was good enough for the MacKenzies:

- 🌍 They went to Amsterdam but found the Dutch tulippy.
- 🌍 They took a slow boat to China but they were bored to death by the time they got there.
- 🌍 They went to Coventry but the locals wouldn't talk to them.
- 🌍 They flew to Warsaw but found it an eyesore.
- 🌍 They found Cuba dull (although everyone else seemed to be Havana good time).
- 🌍 They went to Egypt but the pyramids were like a prism.
- 🌍 They went to Sao Paulo but thought the Brazilians were nuts.
- 🌍 They sailed to Costa Rica but it Costa fortune.
- 🌍 They got hungry in Hungary.

🌐 So they had turkey in Turkey.

🌐 And then chicken in Kiev.

🌐 And crackers in Caracas.

🌐 And visited a Deli in Delhi.

🌐 They got thirsty in Chertsey.

🌐 So they had high tea in Haiti.

🌐 Then drank iced tea in the Black Sea.

🌐 They went for a wander in Rwanda.

🌐 Something went wrong in Hong Kong.

🌐 They weren't bowled over by Moldova.

🌐 They found Chile too cold.

🌐 They bought perfume in Cologne.

🌐 Mr. MacKenzie had a very painful accident in Bangkok.

🌐 They found Nuremberg a trial.

🌐 They thought that Guinea was fowl.

🌐 They went to a party in Toga.

🌐 Things got vicious in Mauritius.

🌐 They saw sea shells sitting in the Seychelles.

🌐 They watched the Gaza Strip.

🌐 They heard the Galway Bay.

🌐 They saw the Colorado Springs.

🌐 They got lost on the way to San Jose.

🌐 They bought new pyjamas in the Bahamas.

🌐 They couldn't settle in Seattle.

🌐 They got catarrh in Qatar.

🌐 It was not so great in Crete.

In the end they simply flew back to France – they had nothing Toulouse.

Back in France Mrs. MacKenzie declared that the rest of the world was boring. That it was dull. That it was overrated. That the food was funny. That in future she'd be taking her holidays back in England. They boarded one final plane and ended up in Weston-Super-Mare. There Mrs. MacKenzie spent a contented week sitting indoors watching the rain and complaining about the English weather, the English food, the price of alcohol, how ugly the tourists were and about how foreigners were taking over our country and should go back to where they belonged.

She smothered herself in fake tan, not forgetting to brown her eyelids. She fed lit cigarettes to the seagulls. She wore a 'Kiss Me Quick' hat that terrified her fellow holidaymakers. She hogged the karaoke machine. She lost hundreds of pounds playing the slot machines on the pier.

She had never been so happy.

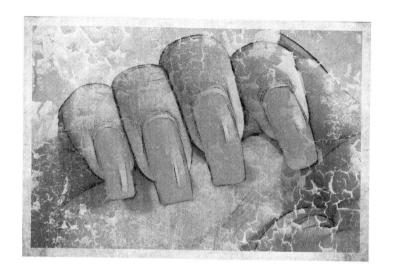

Chapter 11 – Hotel

The days turned into weeks and the weeks turned into months and Felicity MacKenzie turned into a great big walking sack full of money. She left a trail of paper and silver wherever she went. People followed her like seagulls follow sardines being thrown into the sea. Like journalists pursue celebrities on their way to the top. Like celebrities pursue journalists on their way to the bottom. Nothing, it seemed, was too large or too small to avoid being exchanged for a handful of cash by Mrs. MacKenzie.

By now the flat was so crammed full of objects of all shapes and sizes that it was actually impossible to get inside unless you were one of the seven dwarves. The family were left with no choice but to move to a hotel while Mr. MacKenzie decided what to do next. It was, of course, the poshest hotel that Mr. MacKenzie could find. It cost almost £4,000 a night to stay there. And that price didn't include the expensive breakfasts and the expensive dinners that she and her husband Billy regularly tucked into.

This naturally meant that the couple soon put on a great deal of weight. Felicity MacKenzie was now fatter than ever and resembled a clinically obese Sumo wrestler on a reverse hunger strike. Billy MacKenzie was also looking quite podgy but he didn't seem to mind. As soon as he felt his trousers getting too tight he simply threw them away and bought another pair.

The only thing that hadn't really changed was Johnny, who – you know what I'm going to say, don't you – was still wearing the same clothes that he always had. He still wore his dad's shoes and he still looked like he hadn't eaten a decent meal in ages. This was, of course, because he hadn't.

To make matters worse, while his parents were sleeping in a giant four-poster bed, Johnny was sleeping on a camp bed in the corner of the hotel room. His mother explained that this was to 'save money' as they didn't want to waste it on a single room for Johnny.

Every day was a non-stop orgy of buying and Johnny was getting more and more worried. Occasionally he would pick up a discarded receipt from one of the packages that Mr. MacKenzie was opening and his mouth would hang open in horror. His mother was completely out of control and spending money faster than Usain Bolt after an extra hot vindaloo. And during all this time she had never even bought her son one single thing. The injustice of it all made Johnny feel like running away from home. Except that he couldn't because his shoes were too big and he would probably fall over.

Johnny had no idea how much of the £1 million his mother had spent. She held on to the cash card at all times: even when she took a bath or sat on the toilet. When she slept, she kept the card under her pillow.

Occasionally, a letter addressed to Johnny would be delivered to the hotel. More often than not it was quickly picked up by Mr. MacKenzie before Johnny had the chance to open it. But once or twice Johnny had managed to get to the letter before his mother and saw that it was from the bank. He guessed that it was a bank statement telling him how much money he had left in the account that Uncle Marley had set up for him. He was never allowed to see it.

One morning Johnny decided that he would once again ask his mother when she was going to give the card back to him. He caught her in an idle moment when she was sitting in an easy chair in the hotel room having her nails done by a team of six manicurists.

'Mum,' he said.

'What now, Johnny?' sighed Felicity MacKenzie.

'Can I ask a question please?'

Mr. MacKenzie looked at him suspiciously. 'What kind of question?' she asked.

'Well… I was wondering when I could have my cash card back.'

Swatting away the lady doing her nails with the back of her hand, Mr. MacKenzie glared at her son. 'What do you mean 'my cash card'?' she cried.

Johnny looked puzzled for a moment. 'You know,' he replied. 'The cash card that Uncle Marley gave to me… My inheritance.'

'Your inheritance? I think you're very much mistaken my lad!' 'Huh?'

'If you're talking about the cash card that your Uncle Marley left the family in his will. I think you'll find that it's MY cash card.'

'Your cash card?'

'Yes mine. He might have given it to you but it was intended for me. After all, he was my brother. And anyway, you're far too young to be in charge of that amount of money.'

Johnny's mind reeled.

'So from now on you can stop going on about that cash card. It's my – our – cash card. and I'll do what I want with it!'

Johnny tried to think of something to say but he was lost for words. Even so, he wasn't exactly surprised by what his mother had said. Because deep down he had known right from the start that she had no intention of returning the card to him.

He could see from the look in her eye that she now believed that the cash card card was rightfully hers. All the spending and the eating and the drinking had jumbled her mind. If she thought back to the funeral Johnny was sure that his mother would remember that Uncle Marley really did give the card to her.

Johnny left his mother and sat down on his camp bed to think. Something had to be done about his mother's spending. Something had to be done to stop her from wasting his inheritance. Something had to be done to give him a fighting chance of going back to the church and fulfilling Uncle Marley's task.

He just wasn't sure what.

Chapter 12 – Plan #1

Johnny Nothing, as you're sure to have noticed by now, was an easy going, uncomplaining sort of boy. Even though he was the poorest child in school you never once heard him moan about it when his schoolmates came into class wearing smart new clothes. Or when they brought toys in on the last day of term and he brought nothing in at all. When you were used to having nothing it didn't seem worthwhile complaining about it. Nobody would have listened anyway.

Johnny didn't even say much when his bullying mother confiscated Uncle Marley's inheritance and began her spending spree. And he didn't complain when Mrs. MacKenzie proceeded to buy gifts for everyone in the world but him. He didn't say a word when the family moved into a posh hotel and he was given an uncomfortable corner of the room to sleep in.

But the news that Mrs. MacKenzie intended to keep the cash

card for good was the last straw. Something inside Johnny snapped and for one of the few times in his life he felt real genuine anger. It simply wasn't fair that his mother had stolen his inheritance. And it wasn't fair that she was spending it so quickly that he had no chance whatsoever of completing Uncle Marley's task and earning £10 million. It wasn't fair that he seemed to be the only one who wasn't benefitting from the windfall.

At last he decided it was about time that he did something about it.

Johnny spent a sleepless couple of nights thinking what he was going to do next. And then finally he came up with a plan: He was going to take back his cash card. He was going to steal it from his mother. It was not going to be easy. He would have to find a time when she was distracted but he was going to do it.

The obvious time was when she was asleep. But he had noticed that she always kept the card under her pillow. He would have sneak up when she was asleep, carefully slip his hand under his mother's pillow and take it without her noticing. The only problem was that even if he managed to do this, he had no idea what he was going to do next.

Chapter 13 – Dinner

t was early in the morning. The sun had dipped behind the other side of the Earth to take a bit of a breather. The birds were following its example by having a crafty nap themselves. On the empty streets of London the wind whistled tunelessly through piles of rotting rubbish. It seemed like the only person in the whole world who was still awake was Johnny Nothing. He was lying in the corner of the posh hotel room trying not to listen to the colourful assortment of noises that his parents were producing as they grunted, parped and snored their way through the night. Johnny was nervous – he was trying to summon up the courage to carry out **OPERATION CASH CARD**.

Earlier that evening – while Johnny was left to his own devices in the hotel room – his parents had gone out for a meal at an obscenely expensive French restaurant. It was the kind of place where you had to book a year early to have any chance of even setting foot on to the same street. Felicity MacKenzie, however, had simply waved a handful of rustling banknotes in the direction of the manager and a free table had magically materialised. She was getting good at doing this.

Have you ever been to a really posh restaurant? Well if you haven't you should know that the posher the restaurant the more disgusting the food is. It's really true. Cheap restaurants generally have quite edible things on the menu such as sausages, fish fingers, mashed potatoes and chips. The more expensive a restaurant becomes, however, the more the food starts to resemble an *I'm A Celebrity Get Me Out Of Here!* bush-tucker trial.

The really top restaurants actually enjoy getting their customers to eat the most revolting things imaginable. They have chefs with funny names who make you things like raw calf's liver, raw fish and eggs that are three years old and smell like diarrhoea. The staff sit in a back room giggling as people try to force down the most horrible things imaginable. And the owners of these places are not stupid: knowing that diners will be desperate to wash away the taste of the monstrosities they have just consumed, they charge a small fortune for drinks.

Mr. and Mrs. MacKenzie had just visited such a place. While he pretended to enjoy what he was eating, Billy MacKenzie had held his nose as frog's legs, snails and raw beef slithered down his throat. Felicity MacKenzie had been eggy burping through goose liver, raw horse and something slimy in an orange sauce which she couldn't pronounce. They had both followed this with a piddly little piece of apple tart covered in cream that tasted like sick which had been allowed to go off.

The delicate flavour of the meal had been rinsed away with three bottles of red wine that each cost more than the average person's kitchen extension. On the way home, however, the couple had gotten a little peckish for some proper food. So they had stopped the cab at a fish and chips shop to fill up on meat pies and saveloys. It was a fairly normal night for them.

When they got back to the hotel they had called room service and ordered some chocolates and another bottle of wine to take away the taste of the meat pies and saveloys. After gobbling and glugging these down they had retired to bed and quickly slipped into unconsciousness.

While they slept, their stomachs quickly set to work finding a way of getting rid of all the vile things that were swilling about inside them.

Billy MacKenzie – who never had a particularly strong constitution – was soon busy converting his meal into deadly swamp gas. This was ejected from his rear end with a rhythm that was in perfect synch with his breathing. It sounded rather like this: 'Inhale… Parp… Exhale… Parp… Inhale… Parp… Exhale… Parp…' And so on and so forth. To the untrained ear the noise was like a recording of a motorcycle played back at quarter speed. The smell was not too dissimilar.

Mrs. MacKenzie, being larger and louder than her husband, took longer to digest her dinner. As her straining gullet went to work she began to snore. This was no normal snore. If she was a superhero it would have been her special power. The noise was so deafeningly horrific that two floors down a young couple on their honeymoon called room service to ask if a herd of extinct mastodons had escaped from a zoo somewhere.

It was at this moment that Johnny Nothing decided to make his move.

While his parents tossed, turned and trumped Johnny crept stealthily towards their bed. He waited for a moment to check that they really were asleep. The trees rustled outside and he struggled to keep his fingers from trembling as he delicately – oh, so, delicately – slid them under his mother's pillow and fished around for the cash card that he knew was there.

In the movies, of course, in this sort of scene the sleeping person usually stirs and then grabs hold of the person doing the stealing. There is often huge laughs from the audience as the thief is then dragged into bed and cuddled or hugged by the sleeping person.

This didn't happen. Well actually it did.

What happened was that Mrs. MacKenzie stirred a little and then grabbed hold of Johnny and dragged him into bed. He lay there heart beating like a hyperactive bongo player, wrapped in her huge, meaty arms for several moments. The seconds ticked slowly by marked by the 'Inhale… Parp… Exhale… Parp…' of Mr. MacKenzie's breathing.

If Johnny had known that this was going to happen he would perhaps have greased himself up in advance. However, by wriggling his body a tiny little bit at a time he was eventually able to slither away from his sleeping mother's bear hug.

In the movies, of course, what happens next is that sleeping person wakes up temporarily and then says something funny before going back to sleep again.

You guessed it. For some strange reason this is exactly what Mrs. MacKenzie did next. Without warning her eyes popped open and she looked straight through Johnny. Then, for no apparent reason, she yelled 'My **PRECIOUS!**!' and then turned over and went back to her snoring.

Things weren't going exactly to plan but Johnny was determined. He was resolute. He had only one thing on his mind. Once more he moved towards his mother's sleeping torso. In the half-light of the hotel room, the sight of her reminded him of a giant sack of uncooked sausage meat.

The next thing that happened was that Billy MacKenzie suddenly stood up and started sleep walking. If Johnny had been able to climb into his father's mind he would have realised that Billy was actually having a dream about being awake and needing the toilet. In the dream, Mr. MacKenzie wasn't quite sure that he was awake, he thought there might be a chance that he was dreaming. Whatever the case he definitely needed to go to the toilet.

As Johnny looked on Billy stumbled around, blindly searching for the bathroom but with no chance whatsoever of finding it. In the end he bumped into the wardrobe and opened one of the doors and climbed inside. There he spent the rest of the night. In the morning the maid would find herself wondering if the ceiling above the wardrobe had sprung a leak.

While his father did his diabolical deed in the wardrobe, Johnny resumed his efforts at finding the cash card. His mum ground her teeth and restlessly slapped her lips together like a baby demanding a bottle. The sound only made Johnny's heart pound even faster. If she were to wake up and catch him in the act there was no telling what his punishment would be. Life was hard enough for Johnny even when he was behaving himself.

Johnny's fingers continued to fumble around under the pillow. He seemed to do this for hours and hours. He was beginning to think that he had been mistaken, that his mother had perhaps chosen a different hiding place for the cash card. Then, suddenly, his fingers felt something thin and plastic. It was the cash card! Grabbing hold of the object as tightly as he could he gently prised it away from beneath Mrs. MacKenzie's head.

He had the card!

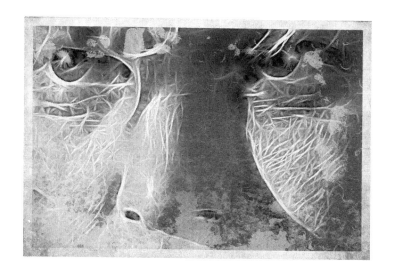

Chapter 14 - Precious

It took a grand total of five seconds for Felicity MacKenzie to realise that the cash card was missing. The clock had just struck 11.00am when Mrs. MacKenzie prised open her eyes, shook her head to grudgingly acknowledge that another day's shopping had begun and immediately fished under her pillow for her beloved cash card. This was something she always did. The card had become the most important thing in her life.

The beginnings of a frown crept on to her face when she realised the card wasn't in its usual place. She immediately hoisted herself upright in bed and lifted her pillow. When she saw that the slim piece of plastic was not there she felt around the back of the mattress. The beginning of the frown turned into a fully fledged frown when she realised that it was not there either.

She thought for a few moments and her pulse rate went up a notch or two. Then she peered under the bed and the frown was replaced by a look of sheer panic as she saw that the cash card was nowhere to be seen.

'Billy! Billy! Wake up!" she cried, urgently shaking her sleeping husband's shoulders.

'I'll have a gin…' said Billy MacKenzie dreamily.

'Billy! Wake up! Wake up!'

'Whatsamatter, Fliss?' Mr. MacKenzie groaned in dismay at being awoken in this crude fashion at such an ungodly hour.

'The card. Billy. Have you got the card?'

'What card?'

'What do you mean "what card?" THE card you idiot!'

'Why would I have the card?' mumbled Billy. Like his son, he was never allowed within six feet of the cash card.

Mrs. MacKenzie got out of bed and picked up a telephone that sat on a desk nearby.

'Gimme room service!' she yelled.

'Hello, my name's Linda. How can I help this fine morning, madam?' said a polite voice.

'Has the maid been cleaning up in here while we were asleep?'

'No I don't think so, madam.'

'Are you quite sure, knucklehead?'

'Let me check.'

Mrs. MacKenzie tutted in frustration as she was placed on hold and the sound of a badly played electropop version of 'Greensleeves' could be heard. Downstairs in the foyer, receptionist Linda was holding an electronic keyboard and grinning to herself as she fumbled her way through a two-fingered version of 'Greensleeves'. 'Another twenty minutes of this will teach her to be so rude,' she thought.

Mrs. MacKenzie put the phone down and screwed her face up into a grimace. Her eyes darted around the room like searchlights. 'Where is it?' she cried. 'Where's my **PRECIOUS?!**'

By this time Billy MacKenzie had managed to drag himself out of bed. His wife's words reminded him of someone he'd seen in a movie but he couldn't recall who.

'Oh my dear God, Billy,' exclaimed Mrs. MacKenzie, clutching her hands to her heart as she spoke. 'We must have left the card in the taxi last night!'

Her husband thought for a moment. 'We can't have,' he said. 'How did we pay for the food in the fish and chip shop?'

'I can't remember,' said Mrs. MacKenzie. 'Last night is just a blur – I just can't remember very much at all.'

For the next 20 minutes Felicity MacKenzie turned the hotel room upside down in her quest for the cash card. The bed was pulled out, the mattress was dragged off the bed and turned over. All cupboards and drawers were roughly hauled open and their contents emptied on to the carpet. Handbags and wallets were ransacked and then discarded in frustration. Soon the whole room looked like it had been decorated by a troupe of angry breakdancing rugby players.

Mrs. MacKenzie sat down on the bed and held her head in her hands. 'My cash card,' she sobbed. 'My lovely, beautiful **PRECIOUS**…'

Then, suddenly, she fell silent as a thought hit her.

And she slowly turned to look at Johnny, giving the thought that had just hit her a slap as she did so.

'You're very quiet,' she said menacingly.

As if to prove her point, Johnny did not answer.

His mum narrowed her eyes and stared at Johnny intently. He felt himself blush.

Have you ever lied to your parents and then been caught out? I'd be very surprised if you haven't tried this at least once in your life. A little bit of advice if you ever try this again and want to avoid being caught. What you must avoid doing is looking away when they ask you a question. Try to look them right in the eyes and do not blink at all costs. Sometimes it helps if you can think of something else when you're doing this; something nice like putting salt in your brother's orange squash or taking a day off school sick. If you can do this you'll stand a fighting chance of getting away with whatever you've done. If you practice you'll find that you are able to get away with literally anything.

Unfortunately, Johnny Nothing had not been practising anything like as much as he should have been. As his mother glared at him there was no other word for how he looked. He just looked guilty. He might as well have been wearing a shirt with arrows printed on it. She knew he was guilty. He knew he was guilty. He was obviously guilty. He was more guilty than a guilty person found guilty of being guilty of cheating in a guilty competition.

'Give it to **ME**,' said Mrs. MacKenzie slowly in a voice that was a whole lot quieter than it really ought to have been. 'Give me my card.'

'What card?' said Johnny foolishly, not looking his mother in the eye and blinking furiously.

'**GIVE. ME. THE. CARD.**'

'What card?' repeated Johnny.

'**GIVE. ME. MY. PRECIOUS!**'

Johnny looked down at his feet. There was no point in carrying on with this charade. She knew. He knew. I knew. You knew. Everybody knew (except Billy MacKenzie, who wasn't sure what he knew). He reached into his pocket and reluctantly handed the cash card back to his mother.

Mrs. MacKenzie clutched the cash card to her chest and

stroked it gently, as if it were a purring kitten. She exhibited her relief in a series of cooing noises that were actually surprisingly pleasant to listen to given the circumstances. Then she took in a deep gulp of air through her nose and began the process of deciding what to do to her errant son.

'How dare you steal **MY** cash card?' she growled. '**MY** cash card!'

Johnny shook his head and said in a very quiet and sorrowful voice: 'Sorry…'

He had half a mind to point out that it was in fact HIS cash card. But he wisely decided against doing so.

'And just what on earth did you think you were going to do with it?' Mrs. MacKenzie asked. 'Did you think that I wouldn't notice that it was gone?'

In truth she had a fair point. For Johnny had laid awake most of the night pondering just those questions. It was all very well managing to steal the card back but once he had it in his possession what was he supposed to do with it?

Even if he wanted to he could hardly go out on a spending spree himself. Likewise, he couldn't just hold on to the card, keep it hidden away. And then expect his mother to just shrug her shoulders and say something like: 'Oh well… Easy come easy go… It was good while it lasted…'

He now realised the folly of what he had done and it made him even more upset and depressed than he had been before he had stolen the card. He was trapped. His mother was just going to go on spending and spending until there was nothing left.

One day soon it would all be gone and they would have to move back into the council flat. The chances of completing Uncle Marley's task were just impossible. He would end up dressed in exactly the same clothes that he had always worn. He'd still have his father's shoes on. And the pupils and the teachers at his school would still call him Johnny Nothing.

This was his life. He had better get used to it.

There was no way out.

The beautiful Felicity MacKenzie
wants to invite you to
the BEST PARTY EVER!

SO YOU'D BETTER COME!!!

Chapter 15 – Party

elicity MacKenzie was so relieved to get her **PRE-CIOUS** cash card back that she decided to celebrate in style. You may remember back in Chapter 09 her husband, Billy, had requested a party. So Felicity decided there was to be a party. And even before Mrs. MacKenzie began to think about who to invite she had already decided that it was to be the party to end all parties.

Now, most of us like a party, don't we? There's balloons. There's jelly. There's games. There's goodie bags. There's cake. What's not to like about parties?

What I'm talking about, however, are children's parties. Grown-up parties are an entirely different kettle of fish.

You may have to wait for a couple of years before you are invited to your first grown-up party. This will probably be when you are a teenager. And you're going to be very excited indeed. Let me tell you what will happen when you get there:

The Teenage Party

The teenage party usually takes place at somebody's house when their parents are away. After asking permission to 'have a few friends around' in their parents' absence, an open invitation to the party will then be posted on Facebook or Twitter. Thousands upon thousands of teenagers will duly respond and attempt to stuff themselves into the house like commuters in a rush hour train.

All of them will smoke cigarettes. But because none of them will have any money they will not be able to afford any cigarettes. Instead, they will smoke anything they can lay their hands on. Substances like tea, bits of dust from under the fridge or cat fluff. All of them will use the carpet as an ashtray – which is usually guaranteed to please the parents when they get home. (Don't smoke kids!)

All of them will drink alcohol. But because none of them have any money they will drink anything they can lay their hands on. Things like aftershave, contact lens cleaning fluid or antifreeze. (Don't drink kids!)

Fights will break out. Someone will get chained to a lamp post in the street. Neighbours will complain. Police will be called.

I'll bet you can't wait, can you? You'll find yourself longing for the days of jelly and cake.

The Grown-Up Party

By the time that you're old enough to be invited to a proper grown-up party you'll probably be married to somebody really dull like everyone else who's been invited.

Not many people will attend the grown-up party, although all of them will have babies strapped to them on special harnesses. They will place these screaming and dribbling balls of poo and sick on parade as if they've won an Oscar for making babies.

Everyone will be able to afford cigarettes and alcohol but nobody will smoke or drink because it might affect the health of the screaming and dribbling balls of poo and sick. (Don't smoke or drink kids!)

Really boring games of charades will be played. Blurry videos of mothers giving birth to balls of poo and sick will be shown. And everyone will leave early just in time to catch the end of the ten o'clock news.

The OAP Party

After you've retired and all your bobbly bits have dropped and your teeth have fallen out and your skin resembles an ordinance survey map you might be unlucky enough to be invited to an OAP[6] party.

In this sort of party it is compulsory to attend whether you want to or not. There, people younger than you will talk to you like they're older than you. And you will be forced to sit on uncomfortable chairs while music from 500 years ago is played.

Jelly will be distributed which you'll suck up through straws. Cake will be served and fed to you while you're wearing a bib. Balloons will be passed around. By the end of the day people will be talking to you like you're a baby and you will be nodding along happily, secretly hoping they will go away.

The Conservative Party

Not much of a party at all.

---

6   OAP. Old And Pathetic

The Posh Person's Party

This is a special type of party that only posh people get invited to. It's a combination of The Teenage Party, The Grown-Up Party and the OAP Party.

Balloons will be distributed – only balloons that are covered in diamonds and imported from Monaco or Brazil or somewhere like that. Slices of dangerously unhealthy cake will be eaten – cut from a cake that is big enough to hide a small family of illegal immigrants inside. Cigars will be smoked (if you've never had one, these are giant-sized cigarettes the colour, smell and taste of horse manure). Wine and cocktails will be drunk. The most expensive food in the solar system will be served and then used to stub cigars out on. And everyone will wake up with an incredibly bad headache and no memory whatsoever of ever having attended a party the night before.

This is the type of party that Felicity MacKenzie wanted.

The Felicity MacKenzie Party

Felicity decided to hire Buckingham Palace for her party. However, when she discovered that the Queen was hosting a garden party on the same day she opted instead for a big posh hotel in the middle of Mayfair (If you've ever played Monopoly you'll know that dark blue Mayfair is the most expensive property on the board and almost always guarantees a win). This was not before she had sent the Queen a very angry letter, telling her she was a 'trollop', an 'ugly old bat' and that Prince Philip had 'breath like old mens' farts'. The Queen was not amused and would have ordered her men to chop off Mrs. MacKenzie's head if only she still had that power.

Having no real friends, Mrs. McKenzie wasn't sure who to invite to the party. Therefore to make sure that enough people came she had invites designed for the entire council estate. These were printed on stiff card in real gold plated letters. There's a picture of one of the invites at the start of this chapter.

To provide food, Mrs. MacKenzie decided she would hire a proper chef off the telly. She contacted Gordon Ramsey (a very successful chef off the telly who suffers from Tourette's Syndrome)[7]. 'Course I'll ******** do it,' he said when she got him on the phone. 'But it will cost you £10,000 ******** quid.'

To provide liquid refreshment she hired a troupe of singing cocktail waiters. They mixed together different types of alcoholic drink to make exotic sounding concoctions with names like 'Fuzzy Naval', 'French Kiss' and 'Sex on the beach'. Although they tasted awful and one sip was enough to knock you off your feet, they each had a cherry on top.

Felicity thought long and hard about what she should do about entertainment for the party. Billy MacKenzie was in favour of hiring someone off the telly like Les Dennis[8] or David Cameron.[9] But Felicity liked to dance so she decided she would hire the Beatles.[10] When it was pointed out that two of the Beatles were actually dead she decided she would hire someone off the X-Factor.[11]

---

7   Tourette's Syndrome. A strange condition that makes sufferers swear continuously. For a bit of fun you might like to pretend that you have the disease and go up to your headmaster and say: 'Oy! *****face! Why don't go and **** yourself and ****** ****** *****!!!' If he gets angry and threatens to put you into detention simply say: 'Sorry **** face. I've got Tourette's Syndrome. Here's a doctor's note. So **** off!!'

8   Les Dennis. Politician from the 1970s

9   David Cameron. Comedian from the 2010s

10   The Beatles. Little known pop group from the 1960s who said 'Yeah! Yeah! Yeah!' a lot.

11   TV shown run by bloke with very high waisted jeans and an Irish bloke with a very realistic looking hairline. Encourages people who can't sing to go on telly and show millions of people that they can't sing and

She remembered that she liked one contestant who couldn't actually speak unless he was singing. He could only stutter. However, when she tracked him down she found that he was busy on the night of the party. By some strange coincidence he was working as a waiter at the very same hotel in which the party was being held and his manager refused to give him time off.

In the end she hired the Rolling Stones,[12] who were mostly alive and remarkably cheap. For a couple of crates of lager and 6,000 packets of cigarettes the band agreed to perform a medley of hits from their heyday in the 1860s.

Just in case, she also hired some Russian ballet dancers; several BAFTA Award winning actors; some bloke off the telly who could hypnotise you into believing you are chickens; Mr. Tumble from Cbeebies; several Tigers from a travelling circus; One Direction; and the entire cast of Eastenders.

Johnny watched in miserable silence as his mother flashed the cash card as if she was waving a fan on a hot summer's day. On the one occasion that he did manage to summon up the courage to question his mother's spending her response was: 'Shut up you little runt! It's my cash card, not yours! What are you gonna do? Steal it again? Just you keep away from my **PRECIOUS!**'

On the night of the party Mrs. MacKenzie wore a new dress that had been especially created for her by a very famous fashion designer called Vivienne Eastwards. It was made from bits of wood and animal teeth knotted together with string. It cost a large fortune. She really did look a picture (if that picture happened to Leonard Da Vinci's lesser-known painting of the Mona

---

then be laughed at.
12   The Rolling Stones. Pre-historic, big-lipped, wrinkly rockers.

Lisa's husband's hairy bottom crack). Billy MacKenzie also had on a very posh suit that was made from real silver. It weighed so much that he had to get two members of One Direction to stop him from falling over. Johnny Nothing – who, surprisingly, had been allowed to come to the party – wore a red jumper and a pair of his dad's old shoes.

The guests began arriving at 8 o'clock sharp. I can't really lie to you here. They weren't a pretty sight.

Most of the guests did not have jobs and, therefore, did not have any money to buy new clothes. The women had on rejects that they had bought from the local marketplace. This meant that some of the blouses they wore had three arms and others had only one. And some of the dresses they wore were ten sizes too small or twenty sizes too big.

The men wore what men always wear to parties: their best suit. By best suit, I mean the only suit they possessed; usually worn for weddings, funerals, christenings, engagement parties and job interviews. Covered in stains and stinking of moth balls.

After cocktails were dished out by very posh waiters wearing bow ties (they also wore suits, stupid! Don't get the idea they were walking around naked except for a bow tie!) the guests sat down to eat. It was very posh food indeed. There wasn't a horse meat hotdog in sight.

There were at least 500 guests present and each of them were treated to a meal of the highest standard. For their starter they were served raw oysters in a sauce made from fresh octopus ink. For the main course they were given crocodile steaks in a bed of rare orchids garnished with the raw intestines of a wild pig that had died in its sleep of natural causes. For pudding they got jelly. Not ordinary jelly but posh jelly made from jelly that had been extracted from the bones of a frozen wooly mammoth. Perhaps surprisingly most people only managed to force down a few mouthfuls of their meal before deciding that they weren't hungry after all and asking if there were any prawn cocktail crisps about.

It might have been nervousness but during all this Felicity MacKenzie consumed rather too many of the cocktails that were being handed out. By the time she had finished her starter she was slurring her speech. Midway through the main course she was getting leery (leery is what adults become halfway to getting completely drunk) and saying nasty things about her neighbours and anyone who happened to be within touching distance. By the pudding so drunk was she that Felicity no longer knew who she was. She couldn't recall that she was a middle-aged woman from a council estate in North London. She thought was a member of the Spice Girls, which clearly wasn't true (unless there was a Spice Girl named Ugly Fat Spice).

She was a spitting and snarling monster, threatening to kiss or punch anyone who came near her. Telling anyone who would listen that she either 'loved them' or 'hated' them.

As the evening drew to a close Mrs. MacKenzie lay face down in a plate of expensive mammoth jelly. To top off the night she had secretly paid for the corpse of Elvis Presley to be dug up. As she lolled about, oblivious to what was happening the dead Elvis was wheeled up to her snoring torso. A chorus of '*Are You Lonesome Tonight*' was then played over the hotel speakers. It was a touching – if somewhat smelly – moment that Felicity MacKenzie never quite got to experience.

Throughout all this Johnny Nothing had been watching in dismay. Although he was seated close to his parents nobody had really noticed him because they were too busy trying to force down the expensive food or watching the expensive entertainment.

Johnny looked at his mother in her expensive designer dress. He watched her mouth open and close in perfect time with the loud Rhino-like snores that were emanating from it. He thought about Uncle Marley and what he might say if he was alive to see how his money was being spent. He thought about Uncle Marley's task – returning to the church a year after the funeral with more than £1 million was obviously completely out of the question.

And then he noticed something.

Hanging around his mother's shoulders was an expensive piece of metal and leather that she called a handbag. He recognised it from their very first trip to Harrods. It had cost a fortune, which was a little absurd because it was as well suited to being used as a handbag as a teabag was. It was so tiny that practically nothing was small enough to fit into it. Except for, perhaps, a cash card.

And there it was for all to see. The cash card – his cash card – was sitting in the stupid handbag. The zip of the handbag was half open. If Johnny reached over he could touch it.

And this is exactly what he did.

After quickly checking that nobody was watching him Johnny leaned over and gently took the cash card from his mother's minute handbag. She didn't stir. She didn't wake up. She just carried on snoring. That was all there was to it.

He had the cash card. It was his.

Checking again to see if anybody was watching him, Johnny got to his feet and left his table. In the corner of his eye he could see a group of Russian ballet dancers jumping around to the strains of the Rolling Stones while the hypnotist off the telly was getting people to behave like chickens. Johnny found the exit of the hotel and quietly slipped away into the night.

Chapter 16 - Escape

Johnny headed for the hotel with the cash card safely tucked away inside his pocket. His plan was to collect a few things and then get as far away from the place as possible before his parents returned from the party.

When he reached the hotel he explained to Linda the receptionist that he didn't have the key to the room and asked if he could borrow a spare. Under normal circumstances Linda would have asked a child as young as Johnny to wait in reception until his parents arrived. However, Linda had been watching the MacKenzie family and could not help but notice how badly neglected Johnny was. She gave him the key with a smile and even asked if he would like her to order him something to eat.

Even though he had just been to the biggest party of his life, Johnny Nothing was ravenously hungry. He had watched in dismay as people sat and stuffed their faces. And yet strangely enough nobody had actually gotten around to offering him any food. It was torture.

'Can I have some jelly?' he asked.

'Of course,' said Linda.

'With bits of sponge in it and a layer of custard?'

'No problem at all, Sir'

'And some cream on top covered in hundreds and thousands?'

'Anything at all,' said Linda, already on the telephone ordering Johnny's concoction.

The food arrived within minutes and Johnny gobbled it down hungrily.

'Thanks so much,' he said, wiping globules of jelly from his mouth.

'Think nothing of it,' replied Linda. 'It's merely a trifle.'

***

Back in the hotel room Johnny frantically began opening drawers and looking in cupboards. He was searching for Uncle Marley's briefcase. He hunted high and low but could find no sign of it. Although he had no trouble at all finding pairs of his dad's baggy underpants that had been abandoned down the sides of chairs or under the bed. And every now and then he would come across bits of old pie crust covered in hair that had been dropped underneath the sofa. But the briefcase stubbornly refused to reveal itself.

Johnny had been searching for about fifteen minutes and

was beginning to get very nervous when he heard the roar of a car pulling up outside the hotel followed by the sound of raised voices. He recognised the voices instantly.

He moved over to a window and drew back the curtain. Three floors below the hotel room his parents could be seen stumbling out of a taxi. Still wearing his silver suit, Johnny's father was yelling instructions at a couple of bellboys, who were gamely trying to lift Felicity MacKenzie's semi-conscious bulk out of the taxi. Johnny's heart began to pound but then something lying at his feet caught his attention. It was made of brown leather and had a shiny silver handle. It was the briefcase! The briefcase that had been given to him at Uncle Marley's funeral! His mother had obviously placed it out of sight behind the curtain. He scooped it up into his arms and charged out of the room.

He reached the lift and saw that it was currently on its way up to the floor that he was on. Johnny was almost certain that the lift contained his parents. He reached the stairs just as the lift opened. Her could hear the familiar sound of his mother snoring, and the grunts of exertion from the unfortunate bellboys who were carrying her like a recumbent hippopotamus with sleeping sickness. Johnny descended the stairs quickly and left the hotel. Linda the receptionist gave him a little wave as he went by.

Johnny now had the cash card and the briefcase but once again he had no idea what to do next. He had until around the mid-morning before his mum awoke and immediately realised that the card was missing. Johnny was sure that she would know that he had taken it. What was he to do?

There were a couple of options: he could find the nearest cashpoint and withdraw some money and then go on the run. Maybe take a train out of London and travel to somewhere

where he couldn't be found. Or perhaps he could stay in the city, book into another hotel somewhere and keep his head down. The problem about both these options was his age. He was simply too young. Someone was bound to notice that he was out on his own and then call the police or something. Then there was his school. He could only be absent for a day or two before his teacher became suspicious and called his parents. What then? He would be a fugitive. On the run and hunted.

It was then that he thought about the briefcase. Inside the briefcase were the objects that Uncle Marley had left him. These included the cash card, an address book and a mobile phone. Johnny found himself recalling what his Uncle had said at the funeral:

'I've instructed Ebenezer to give you assistance should you ever need it. You can call him at any time – night or day – if you need any advice or even if you just want someone to talk to.'

That's what he would do. He would telephone the strange man who was at the funeral and ask for help. With any luck the man would be sympathetic and not take him straight back to his parents.

Johnny pulled the mobile phone from the suitcase and examined it. After a few moments he found what he was looking for – the power switch. He flicked it into the 'on' position and waited. In his mind he tried to remember how long ago the funeral had taken place. Since that morning they had been on holiday, there had been the party, there had been the endless shopping sprees. It had to be several months. Surely the phone would be dead by now?

Johnny held his breath as he watched the object slowly spring back into life. A green light appeared on the screen of the phone. Numbers and letters appeared. Then... Nothing. The phone suddenly went black. It was out of power. Again he felt around inside the briefcase. His fingers found the charger. He had to find a way of charging the phone.

He walked for a while and found himself on a busy high street. There was the usual array of shops: shops selling brightly coloured clothing that only fit really skinny people, the odd book shop, a giant Apple Store filled with people with glazed zombie-like expressions, several hundred coffee shops. And about a thousand gazillion shops selling mobile phones.

He decided the best thing to do was simply ask. He would go into one of these shops and ask if he could charge the phone for a few moments. That was all he would need. He only needed to to make one call.

There is golden rule about going into shops of any kind: if you walk into a shop intending to actually buy something you can be sure that you will be totally ignored – shop assistants will look straight through you or look at you as if you are carrying the Ebola virus. They will ensure that they never come within twenty feet of you. If, however, you go into a shop simply to browse. Just to take a look at what's on offer. To fiddle with the gadgets and set off the odd alarm here and there. You will find that you are immediately surrounded by dozens of shop assistants offering help and telling you what a nice day it is even if it's raining.

This is exactly what happened to Johnny when he walked into the first mobile phone shop that he found. The shop was called something like '**MOBILE-PHONEZ-4-U-4-EVER-U-PAY-US-4-EVER-DUMMY**'. Whatever it was called Johnny didn't understand it.

It was as if he was suddenly invisible. Shop assistants came close to him and sniffed the air suspiciously like dark riders looking for Frodo Baggins but seemed to walk right through him.

He tried coughing to attract their attention. He tried tugging at sleeves. He tried setting off the odd alarm here and there. But nobody noticed him.

Finally, he walked up to the main counter where a **BORED** looking middle-aged woman was being shown a selection of shiny square objects and waited. A LONG TIME.

Eventually, a soiled white shirt wearing a spotty teenager edged towards him and offered a few garbled words: 'My name's Brian.… Can I help you… Sir'. There was a hesitation before the word 'Sir' because Brian wasn't sure if he was dealing with a child, a very small adult or a strange beardless dwarf.

'I don't want to buy anything…'

'Oh…' said Brian in a strange robotic voice.

'…I just wondered if you'd let me charge this mobile phone for a couple of minutes,' said Johnny, gesturing towards the lump of shiny metal and plastic that he was holding.

Brian looked puzzled for a moment. He had not been trained for this eventuality and was nonplussed. 'Have you thought about swapping it for the G17B?' he asked in a dull monotone. 'It's got 3G, 4G, mini-USB, 64GB, 10MP, Edge, Retina and it's a nice shade of blue with a shiny bit on the top.'

'No thanks,' replied Johnny. 'I really only wanted to charge this.'

'I'll check.'

Brian went off to the nearest counter and spoke to an older shirt that was cleaner and more nicely pressed than his. They both looked over at Johnny and exchanged a few words. Then the older shirt got on the phone to another shirt at a call centre in Mumbai. This person spoke to his supervisor who called the manager who paged the CEO who sent an email to the chairman of the shareholder's committee.

There was a delay of about an hour. Finally Brian trudged wearily over to Johnny. 'Yes,' he said. 'But only if we can put you on our mailing list.'

Chapter 17 – Phone

Johnny quickly moved away from the noisy high street and found a quiet park. He was already concerned that his parents might be looking for him and wanted to stay away from main streets. He pulled out the mobile phone and switched it on. After a few moments it glowed sleepily into life. The power meter at the top showed two bars out of a possible five. He had not used this type of mobile phone before but it was fairly easy for him to work out because he was under thirty.

Unlike most modern mobile phones this one simply made phone calls. It did not organise your life. It was not a games station. You did not have to be a freaky genius in order to use it. It did not make cups of tea. It just made phone calls.

Even so, it was still the sort of phone that your parents buy for your grandparents, quietly relieved in the knowledge that they'll never be able to work out how to use it and, therefore, never bother them in the middle of *Coronation Street*.

Johnny fiddled with some of the buttons and his fingers soon found the address book. There was only one name in the address book: 'Ebenezer Dark'. Johnny quickly pressed the call button.

The phone rang a couple of times and an automated response in a droning metallic voice that might have been a female dalek could be heard:

'You have reached Ebenezer Dark and Co Solicitors,' it announced. 'Press '1' on your keypad if you would like to settle our really exorbitant fee. Press '2' if you would like to divorce your wife. Press '3' if you would like to divorce your husband. Press '4' if a really rich relative is just about to die. Press '5' if you are really rich and about to die. Press '6' if you would like to sue somebody. Press '7' if somebody is suing you. Press '8' if you would like to hear all these choices again so that you can be charged twice as much for this phone call. Press '9' if your name is Johnny MacKenzie.'

Johnny frowned. For a moment he did not understand the significance of the last choice. It had been so long since anybody had called him by his real name that he had almost forgotten it. Then he took a step backwards in surprise. He pressed '9' on the keypad.

The phone began to ring again, although it was a different kind of dialling tone than before. It sounded a little like an alarm. Within moments he could hear a voice.

'Mmmmpppphhhhh…' it said in a flustered kind of way. 'Er… Yes… Can I help you?'

'Hello,' said Johnny. 'My name's Johnny Nothing… I mean MacKenzie.'

'Hello Johnny,' said the voice after a moment of silence. 'This is Ebenezer Dark speaking. I've been waiting for your call. What took you so long?'

'Erm… I'm in a bit of trouble.'

'Yes, I thought you might be. What appears to be the problem?'

'It's the cash card.'

'Erm… The cash card. I dare say you're going to tell me that your delightful mother has confiscated it?'

'That's right.'

'And she's been using it to purchase everything she can lay her hands on?'

'That's right.'

'And she won't let you go anywhere near it?'

'Yes.'

'Erm… I fully expected that this might happen. Where are you now?

'I'm in the centre of London.'

'Good. Listen carefully. This is what I want you to do. I want you to hail the first taxi that you see and tell the driver to take you to my office. I'll pay the fare at my end. You still have the briefcase?'

'Yes.'

You'll find my address in the address book.'

'OK.'

'You and I need to have a very long and very serious talk…'

Chapter 18 – Temper

elicity MacKenzie was in an evil mood. She was spitting venom. She was mad as a hornet. She was as crabby as a crustacean. She was like a tiger with its tail on fire. She was a killer gorilla. She was frothing at the mouth like a dolphin cleaning its teeth. She was like a hungover bunny rabbit with a cob on. (OK so the last couple didn't work too well.) The hotel room resembled the most ill-tempered zoo you can possibly imagine. Or perhaps it was an agitated ark. Or maybe a moody menagerie.

For almost two days she had been searching for the missing cash card. Just like the last time she had reduced the hotel room to a pile of dusty rubble in a doomed effort to find it. Even she didn't know why she had done this. Because you didn't need to be Sherlock Holmes in order to realise that the card had gone missing and that Johnny had also gone missing and then put two and two together. Even Doctor Watson wouldn't have needed a calculator to have worked this one out. She wanted that boy – dead or alive.

It was now almost 48 hours since Johnny had disappeared. Most normal parents would have been overcome with worry by now if one of their children had gone missing for that amount of time. But not Mrs. MacKenzie. She couldn't care a hoot about her only child. She just wanted the cash card. Without the cash card her life was over. She wanted it back. She was prepared to kill to get it. 'Wheeerrreeesss my **PRECIOUS!**' she wailed mournfully.

Beside her was Billy MacKenzie. He was keeping as quiet as he possibly could. He knew that drawing attention to himself when his wife was in this kind of mood was rather like putting your hand in a fish tank full of starving pirañas that had a particular liking for Billy MacKenzie flavoured fingers. He, too, had had a pretty sleepless couple of nights. His wife had been tossing and turning and hissing relentlessly. It had been like sharing a bed with a sackful of angry ferrets. The smell she had been giving off was pretty similar, too.

It was getting on for midday when the phone suddenly rang. 'Yes!' yelled Mrs. MacKenzie into the receiver, hoping that the call would bring news of her beloved cash card.

'Good morning madam, this is Linda the receptionist,' said Linda the receptionist. 'I have a message for you.'

'Is it about my missing cash card?'

'Why yes, madam,' replied Linda politely. 'Actually it is.'

'Spit it out then, birdbrain!'

'One moment please while I locate the message.'

Mrs. MacKenzie was put on hold and Linda's voice was replaced by the sound of 'Greensleeves' played in a Mariachi style.

Downstairs in reception Linda was waving a baton about, conducting a Mexican Mariachi band as they played their own unique version of 'Greensleeves'. 'Let's take the tempo down a bit please, boys,' she said. 'This will teach **HER** to be so rude.'

An hour or so later Linda returned to the phone. 'Sorry for the delay,' she said to an apoplectic Mrs. MacKenzie. 'I had a little trouble finding the message. I don't know who it's from. It says: "**THE CASH CARD IS AT HOME**"'.

Mrs. MacKenzie already had her coat on before Linda had finished that last sentence. Dragging Billy MacKenzie behind her she slammed shut the hotel room door in rage. 'Just wait until I get my hands on that boy!!' she bellowed.

Chapter 19 – Twins

Mr. and Mrs. MacKenzie were out of the hotel fasterthanthis. But when they reached the council flat Johnny was nowhere to be seen. Furthermore, as soon as they looked around them it became obvious that a startling transformation had occurred in the flat during the time that they had been away.

For one thing, the boxes and packages and discarded gifts that had made the flat look like your bedroom does just before your parents threaten to beat you to a pulp if you don't clean it had been removed. They were nowhere to be seen. For a moment Mrs. MacKenzie decided that the flat must have been burgled. However, if this was true then the person who did it had to be the cleanest burglar in the history of domestic crime.

The flat was immaculate. It had never looked so good. The carpets had been vacuumed and shampooed. The paintwork had been scrubbed clean and retouched. If it was a burglar that had done this it had to be a very house-proud burglar. It was as if they had been burgled by Mary Poppins. The flat was cleaner than an episode of '*Songs Of Praise*'.

For one of the few times in her life, Mrs. MacKenzie was lost for words. Her mouth, so used to hogging the limelight, did not know what to do with itself and felt a little self-conscious. Out of frustration it took a nibble out of its owner's bottom lip. 'Ouch!' exclaimed Mrs. MacKenzie.

Mrs. MacKenzie frowned and for a moment thought about giving her mouth a whack back in retaliation. Then she said in her best working class accent: 'Wot's been 'appenin here? Looks like someone's spent weeks cleaning.' Unbeknownst to her, however, this transformation had actually taken place within the last two days.

The couple moved into the kitchen and found it to be equally spotless. Mrs. MacKenzie idly opened a cutlery drawer as if half expecting Johnny to be hiding inside it but found nothing except sparkling knives and forks.

She turned to her husband: 'I can't remember hiring a cleaner,' she said dreamily. Although in truth the past few months had been such a blur that she could scarcely remember anything that she had done.

But Billy was not listening. He was distracted. He thought that he heard movement upstairs. 'Shhhh…' he said, quietly pointing his eyes towards the ceiling. 'Can you hear something, Fliss?'

Mrs. MacKenzie rubbed her hands together and her mouth formed itself into an evil grin, which made it feel a lot better about itself. 'So that's where he's hiding,' she snarled. 'I'll teach that little runt to steal my **PRECIOUS!**'

With her husband close behind her, Mrs. MacKenzie climbed

the stairs and swung open the door to Johnny's room. This had also undergone something of a makeover. It, too, was clean and freshly painted. A new desk had been installed, behind which sat Johnny Nothing. He had a pile of papers in front of him as if he was working in an office. There was a calculator close by.

In an ideal world, Mrs. MacKenzie would have liked to have demanded to know exactly what her son had been up to in the flat. However, when she saw what else was in Johnny's room she temporarily lost the power of speech.

It wasn't the fact that Johnny had nicked her beloved cash card that made her lose her voice. Nor was it that he had run off with the card and then gone AWOL for several days. It wasn't that somebody had broken into the flat and then for some strange reason decided to decorate it. All of these things were currently troubling Mrs. MacKenzie more than she had been troubled in quite some time. But what was really bothering her were Bill and Ben.

Bill had a shaven head and was wearing a blue tracksuit. He was almost seven feet tall and built like an outdoor toilet made of brick. Bill didn't realise this but he was a distant descendent of Neanderthal Man. He had only one eyebrow – one long bushy eyebrow that reached right across his forehead. He looked like what you might get if you force fed a member of Oasis with a half-tonne black plastic sackful of steroids.

And if you were brave enough to be present when he took off his tracksuit you would discover that his back was so covered in hair that he was able part it with a comb. If Bill had had more of an interest in fashion, he might even have considered giving it a curly perm and perhaps a few extensions

On his right arm, Bill had a tattoo which simply read 'Bill'. This was in case he woke up one morning and forgot who he was.

This was actually less unlikely than you might imagine because standing next to him was his twin brother. His name was Ben and he was identical to Bill in every way except that the tattoo on his arm read 'Bin' (the tattooist was either South African or not a very good speller). He was wearing a red tracksuit.

Bill gave Mr. and Mrs. MacKenzie the tiniest of smiles and managed to grunt 'hello'. Ben gave the couple exactly the same tiniest of smiles and also managed to grunt 'hello'.

The two men were standing protectively close to Johnny. They were so large that in the confines of Johnny's bedroom they looked like giants, which they were. They were so enormous that each of them had their own postcode. They were so gigantic that they had their passport photos taken by satellite. They were so humungous that you could spend all day thinking up rubbishy jokes about how big they were and never adequately describe just how indescribably, earth-shatteringly **ENORMOUS** they were. By no stretch of the imagination could you call them small (unless, of course, you were a lot bigger than them).

The pair of Goliaths were having to stoop slightly so as to avoid head-butting the ceiling, which actually even looked a little scared itself. They were a terrifying sight. Even scarier than a school trip to a Weight-Watcher's nudist camp.

There was a long, pregnant silence in the room like this:

This eventually gave birth to an even longer post-natal silence, which, in the interest of preserving the rain forests or the battery on your Kindle, I shan't demonstrate.

The four grown-ups eyed each other nervously. Bill and Ben looked at the Mackenzies like they were looking at insects that could be squashed into pulpy insect juice any time they so desired.

The Mackenzies looked at Bill and Ben like they were looking at two giant skinhead Neanderthal bully boys who had just appeared from nowhere in their recently and unexpectedly decorated council flat.

Johnny looked a little scared.

Finally Billy Mackenzie managed to get his mouth working a little and spluttered: 'Who are you?' And then: 'What do you want?'

There was another long silence – let's call it a pause – while Bill and Ben looked at each other as if trying to decide who was going to answer. Finally Bill spoke: 'You the boy's parents?' he demanded in a voice that sounded like an angry rhino with horn-ache. Although if he was clever enough he would have realised that this was a rhetorical question.

There was yet another long silence (you'll be relieved to hear that this is the last silence you're going to get in this chapter) before Billy Mackenzie mumbled 'Yes'.

'We're Johnny's bodyguards,' continued Bill. 'We're here to make sure that everything's hunky dory.'

'Hunky dory?' Mrs. Mackenzie suddenly found her voice. 'What do you mean 'hunky dory"?'

Now Ben spoke: 'What my brother means to say,' he explained. 'Is that we've been – how shall I say – contracted – to make sure that this young feller's affairs are in order.'

'Get out of my house!' interrupted Mrs. Mackenzie, suddenly feeling a little braver, although she had no idea why.

Bill and Ben looked at each again for a moment. They did this almost as much as your mum looks in the mirror. Or you dad looks at websites that he shouldn't be looking at. 'First of all,' said Bill, 'This isn't a house – it's a flat.'

'And second of all,' said his brother. 'We ain't going nowhere. And neither are you.'

'Johnny who are these men?' Mrs. MacKenzie asked her son, ignoring the two giants.

'I'm sorry mum but…' Johnny started to speak but Bill cut in like a pair of scissors that chops sentences into bits.

'…What the young feller means to say is that the fun's over.'

'The fun's over?' repeated Felicity MacKenzie numbly.

'That's right,' continued Ben. 'You've had a right old time. You've been spending his money like it's your own. You've been ripping the poor young feller off. And we're here to put a stop to it. From now on things are gonna be different.'

'I've had enough of this,' said Mrs. MacKenzie. 'Nobody speaks to me like this in my house…'

'Flat,' corrected Ben.

'Nobody speaks to me like this in my flat. Billy, call the police!'

As usual Billy MacKenzie did as he was told. He reached into his pocket for his mobile phone. Before he had the chance to even turn it on the gigantic frame of Bill was towering over him.

'That an iPhone?' asked Ben.

'Erm… Yes,' said Billy, who could only watch as the huge man took it from him and with one hand crushed it into a chunk of buckled metal and shattered touch screen.

'I think it's broken,' said Ben. 'You ought to take it back to the Apple store. Tell 'em that you're not getting a decent signal.'

'Right!' cried Mrs. MacKenzie. 'We're leaving! You'll be very sorry you did that. I'll fetch the police myself!'

Now the giant frame of Bill was standing in front of her. He was holding something in his hand that looked a little like a child's toy space gun.

'Know what this is?' he asked. Although once again he wasn't clever enough to recognise that this was a rhetorical question.

Mrs. Mackenzie regarded the object for a moment. Then she shook her head. Whatever it was she guessed that it was not intended to provide pleasure, happiness or fulfilment. Anything that has a trigger and a barrel and goes 'bang!' seldom does.

'Come on Billy!' she said. 'We're leaving!'

Bill stood in front of her blocking the doorway. 'Not so fast,' he said, not so slowly. 'It's called a Taser. See this little trigger at the front? If I press this it'll give you a small electric shock. It won't hurt you…Well not too much anyway.'

Bill raised the object and gently touched Mrs. MacKenzie on the arm. There was a loudish bang and a flash of blue neon light and Mrs. MacKenzie collapsed groaning to the floor. She was conscious but wasn't able to move her arms and legs

'Oh my gawd!' said Billy Mackenzie bravely charging out of the room in terror. He got as far as the stairs before there was a second flash. He, too, crumpled to the floor. Bill dragged him back into the bedroom by the scruff of his neck.

Johnny Nothing got to his feet and stood over his two parents. He looked anxious. 'Are they… Are they… OK?' he gasped.

'Don't you worry yourself,' smiled Ben. 'Give em a few minutes and they'll be right as rain.'

'But they'll think twice before they try to run off again,' said his brother.

Chapter 20 – Prison

Felicity MacKenzie and her husband were sitting in their bedroom feeling rather sorry for themselves. In common with the rest of the flat, this room had also enjoyed something of a makeover since the last time they were there.

It was not a big room. There was just about enough space for a double bed, a wardrobe and a small table. In their absence, however, someone had managed to squeeze in a mini fridge and a small cooker. They were similar to the ones you take with you when you go camping. Whoever had placed them there obviously thought that the occupants of the bedroom were going to be staying for some time.

There was also a lock on the bedroom door. Not on the inside to keep people out. But on the outside to keep people in. Somebody had also had a little sliding hatch cut into the door, so that the inhabitants of the room could be observed.

The two adults had barely spoken to each other since Bill and Ben had forcefully shoved them into their bedroom almost an hour ago. They were too shocked and surprised. Who can blame them really? The couple had been frisked and Mrs. MacKenzie's mobile phone had been confiscated. So now they had no way of speaking to anyone from the outside world.

Mrs. MacKenzie was sobbing a little and jabbering on about her '**PRECIOUS**' when she heard the bedroom door open and saw Bill and Ben enter, followed closely by their son. Johnny was carrying a little white envelope. He smiled weakly when he saw his parents.

'Hope you've had time to settle back into your bedroom,' said Bill.

'It ain't much,' said Ben. 'But we've tried to make it cosy as we can…'

'…Cos you're gonna be staying here for some time,' continued Bill, looking over at Johnny. 'Ain't that right, Johnny?'

Johnny looked sheepishly at his parents and nodded meekly.

Through tearstained eyes Mrs. MacKenzie returned the look. 'We're prisoners,' she said mournfully. 'How can a son of mine do this to me?'

'You ain't prisoners,' said Bill. 'How can you be prisoners in your own home?'

'Bill's right,' confirmed Ben. 'You can't be prisoners in your own home.'

'But you won't let us leave,' said Billy MacKenzie.

'Oh, you can leave,' announced Bill. 'You just can't leave right at this very moment.'

Ben turned to face Johnny. 'About time you gave 'em the rules,' he said. 'Come on Johnny – don't be shy.'

Johnny Nothing cleared his throat. Hardly able to look at his parents he began to speak:

'After I took the cash card I went to see Ebenezer Dark…' he said.

'You little thief!' yelled his mother. 'How dare you steal my **PRECIOUS!**'

'Shut up!' said Bill. In his hand he held the Taser. He tapped it menacingly.

'…I told him about how you had taken the cash card and refused to give it back to me…'

'You little sneak!' exclaimed Mrs. MacKenzie.

'Quiet!' ordered Ben in a menacing voice.

'…I told him about how you've been spending lots and lots of money. About the holiday, the hotel, the party…'

'You little rat!' cried guess-who.

'Last warning,' said Bill, holding up the Taser upright and pointing it menacingly towards Mrs. MacKenzie.

'He called Bill and Ben here. He said they were to look after me. Get rid of all the things you bought. Get the place deco-rated so we could live here properly. Stop you from having the cash card. Stop you from spending all the money…

'…He said that you had to move back into the flat. He said that Bill and Ben should keep you here until… Until…'

Johnny's voice trailed off and Ben took over:

'…Until we found out how much money you've spent. And until we can think of a way of getting that money back,' ex-plained Ben.

'You can't be trusted,' said Bill. 'So we're keeping you here until Johnny's managed to get back all the money that you've spent. No more shopping. No more fancy meals. No more go-ing to the betting shop or pub.'

'You little traitor!' cried Mr. MacKenzie. There was a flash of blue light and he collapsed to the floor moaning.

'I warned you!' said Bill, wielding the Taser.

'See that envelope that Johnny's holding?' continued Ben. 'That's a bank statement. Mr. Dark ordered it from the bank this morning. It's gonna tell us exactly how much of that £1 million is left…'

The adults watched as Johnny eased open the envelope. Inside was a small slip of paper folded in two. Johnny pulled it out and ran his eyes over it. 'Oh my word…' he said.

The room grew still, except for the groaning of Billy MacKenzie on the carpet.

'Oh gosh…' said Johnny.

Four pairs of eyes stared at Johnny. That's eight eyes in total but only six eyebrows.

'How much?' said Bill.

'How much?' said Ben.

'How much?' said Mrs. MacKenzie.

'Owww!!!' groaned Mr. MacKenzie.

Johnny looked at the grown-ups and once more cleared his throat. 'It says here that there's £510,000 left in the bank account.'

He turned towards his mother. She looked away guiltily as her son did a quick calculation. 'It means that you've spent £490,000,' he said.

The room fell silent. (Sorry about that. I did say that there wouldn't be another silence.)

The only noise that could be heard was Billy MacKenzie slowly climbing to his feet, the feeling gradually returning to his legs.

'Four-hundred-and-ninety-thousand-quid,' said Bill. 'Spending that much money takes some doing!'

Without warning Billy Mackenzie snatched the Taser out of

Bill's hands. He held it aloft in front of the taller man for a few moments. However, instead of using it on Bill, he turned towards Felicity MacKenzie. There was a further flash of light and Mrs. MacKenzie fell yowling to the floor.'

'Stupid woman!' grumbled Billy, dropping the Taser to his feet.

Chapter 21 – Routine

This is a bit of a tricky chapter because it takes place at the same time as other things are happening in the story. It's called a sub-plot. It's a story that lives in its own little bubble tucked safely away from everything else. It's about what happens to Johnny's parents while he's busy trying to think of a way of getting back all the money that his mother has spent.

As you know, Johnny's only got three months. And nearly half a million quid is a lot of money to try and earn back in only three months. And having a mother (and father) who are only interested in spending that money is not really awfully helpful. So that's why Mr. Dark suggested that it might be a good idea if a means could be found of keeping Mr. and Mrs. MacKenzie out of harm's way for a while.

One suggestion was to kidnap the couple and dump them in the middle of nowhere without any money. Another was to tie them up and give them to an evil fairground owner who would put them on permanent display in the ghost train. Bill and Ben thought that perhaps they could be locked in the boot of a car for a couple of months. All of these ideas held promise but were rejected as being either too stupid or too mean.

In the end it was decided that the safest – and most humane – way of ensuring that they didn't get up to any mischief was to lock them up in their bedroom.

Have you ever tried locking your parents in their bedroom for a couple of months? It is, of course, highly illegal to do this. But it's also tremendous fun. It's an ideal way of teaching them a lesson for not letting you stay up late to watch TV, or making you eat healthy proper food instead of a more tasty diet of sweets and crisps.

It also takes a little planning. You can't just lock them up and throw away the key. You have to give them things to do and things to eat. You don't want them dying of boredom or starvation. Do you?

Do you?

For his part Mr. Dark insisted that Mr. and Mrs. MacKenzie have some means of feeding themselves. That's why the room was equipped with a fridge and a kettle. He also wanted to ensure that they had some form of entertainment. What form this took was left to Johnny. He decided that they shouldn't have a TV because it was not healthy to watch too much television. Instead he took some books out from the library by people like Charles Dickens and Robert Louis Stevenson.

Mr. and Mrs. MacKenzie did a lot of banging about on the first day of their imprisonment. They understandably did not like being confined to their bedroom like naughty teenagers. Mrs. MacKenzie cried like a baby for her **PRECIOUS**. In a gesture of support Mr. MacKenzie also cried like a baby. Mrs. MacKenzie hammered on the door shouting: 'Let me out you little runt! You'll be sorry when you do!' Fortunately, Bill and Ben were always on hand to silence the couple with a few well-placed menacing threats.

Later that evening Johnny took a look at his parents through the hatch that had been cut into their bedroom door. They were asleep but awoke almost immediately and began shouting obscenities and threats at him. They were like a pair of rabid dogs. Johnny decided that they needed to be tamed.

Try to put yourselves in Johnny's shoes: all his life he had been bossed around by his rude and abusive parents. All right, his father wasn't that bad. He might not have called Johnny by his actual name but at least he didn't shout too much. He was more concerned with going to the pub and putting losing bets on horses. But his mother, well, she was another matter.

Deep down Johnny had always known that he wasn't really wanted. It wasn't the fact that he was never given the ordinary simple things that people give to their children such as Christmas presents or birthday presents. And it wasn't the fact that he wore clothes to school that were practically rags. He could have put up with all of this if he had known that his mum and dad wanted him. But they didn't. He was sure of that. He was an inconvenience to them. He was worse than an unwanted pet. He was a liability. And he felt alone in the world. He always had really.

But now, all of a sudden, he had power over his parents. He was in charge of every aspect of their lives. He was their jailer. He could do whatever he wanted to them. And the evil part of his personality – we've all got an evil part, you know (even you) – temporarily took over.

First of all, Johnny decided that his parents would start their day bright and early. An alarm was placed at their bedside that went off each morning at 5.30am. This was no good, however, because his mother quickly stamped on it and smashed it into pieces on the first morning. Another alarm was then placed outside their room that sounded like a fog horn. Each morning Mr. and Mrs. MacKenzie practically jumped out of their skins when it went off. It was not a pretty sight, but an amusing one if you needed cheering up.

Johnny also decided that his parents would eat healthily. They had eaten and drank so much over the past few months that they both resembled walking buckets of lard. For this reason their usual breakfast of fried bacon and sausages with a side helping of beef dripping was replaced by muesli. Of course, they both spat this onto the carpet when they first tasted it but after three or four days of eating nothing else they grudgingly began accepting it.

Likewise they eventually began to eat the salads that they were given for lunch and dinner. They were allowed no alcoholic drinks, they were allowed no sweets, chocolates or crisps. They were miserable and hungry but within a week the weight began to fall off them.

Johnny also demanded that they read the books that he put in their room. To make sure that they did he would set them homework in the evening, which they hated just as much as you do. Johnny insisted that they took this seriously. He gave them books on maths and literacy and punished them if they did not answer the questions properly. Punishment took the form of an early night in bed or, if they had behaved especially poorly, a prod from Bill's Taser. If they did badly in their tests the lights were turned out in the room by 7.30pm. Needless to say this made them even more unhappy.

Bill and Ben watched all of this with amusement. 'It's like he's the parent and they're the kids,' said a laughing Bill.

This was, however, not strictly true. Because in reality the twin bodyguards had actually become the parents that Johnny had never had. They didn't know this but Johnny quickly grew to like them being there. He felt warm and reassured by their friend-ly presence. And they, too, began to like the young boy more and more. They liked his shyness, they liked the way he always greeted their arrival with a smile. And they loved the way he was getting his own back on his parents.

Mr. and Mrs. MacKenzie's life was bleak and desolate. They saw no sunlight and they breathed in no fresh air. They were bored and hungry. The days of their crazy spending spree and limitless cash were just a memory.

Soon they lost track of time. Days slipped into night and nights slipped into days. They could have been there for months. Or they could have been there for years. They had no way of know-ing. Occasionally they would pick out voices talking downstairs when Mr. Dark visited. Sometimes they heard Bill and Ben laughing to themselves as they shared a joke. Every day was the same. Every night was the same.

They got up early. Ate breakfast. Read. Ate lunch. Did their homework. Ate Dinner. Went to bed.

They got used to the routine. It became their lives.

And then one day something unusual happened.

It was late afternoon and Mrs. Mackenzie was lying on the bed dreaming about eating pork scratchings. Her husband lay beside her dreaming about beer and cigarettes. Suddenly, with-out warning, there was a loud commotion outside the flat. In their locked up bedroom the MacKenzies awoke with a jolt.

They could hear dozens – no hundreds – of voices shouting. The sound was tremendous. It was deafening. The couple put their fingers in their ears to shut out the noise. After such a long time spent in silence the sound was amplified tenfold, a hundredfold. The voices were in unison. They were shouting a name. The were shouting: 'Johnny! Johnny! We want Johnny Nothing!'

Chapter 22 – Handbags

Ebenezer Dark was having a dream about the instructions that he had given to Johnny Nothing a day or so earlier when the youngster had visited his office. It was both a convenient and an inconvenient dream.

It was convenient because it gives me the ideal opportunity to do a movie-style flashback and let you know exactly what was said to Johnny in his office on the day in question. It was inconvenient because Mr. Dark was currently sitting in the driver's seat of his car, which, even more inconveniently, was hurtling down the motorway very, very quickly indeed.

To make matters worse, sitting behind the wheel of a small mini and hurtling very, very quickly indeed in the opposite direction was a young lady named Minnie Driver. To make matters worse she was mini driving on the wrong side of the motorway. Silly moo, don't you agree?

What's the chances of this but Minnie was also a solicitor and she was also asleep and having a dream about a ten-year-old boy named Ronny who had visited her for advice only the other day? In actual fact, Ronny was the star of another book called 'Ronny Everything' and his parents had just stolen HIS cash card in order to stop HIM from spending all the wonga. Funny old world, isn't it?

It's an absolutely amazing coincidence – I'm not denying it – and opens up all sorts of exciting possibilities for sequels prequels, cross-pollination of story-lines, Ebenezer and Minnie falling in love and getting married, etc. etc. But…

Bang!

Actually, that bang is simply not loud enough to describe the truly ear-splitting noise that the two motorcars produced when they crashed into each other head-on. Let's try all caps and a couple of exclamation marks:

BANG!!

Still not good enough.

How about a nice illustration to demonstrate just how loud that bang was?

That's better. Although if you're reading the interactive version of this book press the button to the left labelled 'BANG!!' and you'll get an even better idea of the ear-splitting noise that the crash produced. For still more fun, wait until your dad's having a snooze on the sofa and hold your iPad or Kindle up to his waxy earhole and press the button. Write and tell me what happens.

I don't know if you've ever experienced having a dream in the middle of a car crash and then waking up to find that you were dead. I can't say it's happened to me much lately. But if you haven't I can tell you that it really is confusing. In fact, when Ebenezer and Minnie awoke from their dreams to find themselves dead, their level of confusion was simply off the confusion scale.

The first thing that they noticed was that they were floating a good ten or twelve feet above the wreckage of their smashed up vehicles. This is what happens when you die — ask a teacher. You leave your body and float away into infinity. At least, that's what I read somewhere I think. Looking down they could see their mashed up bodies sitting motionless in the respective driver's seats of their mangled cars. It looked like an explosion in a tomato ketchup factory that had been sprayed with zombie gore.

The next thing they noticed was each other. And out of politeness they both gave each other a friendly little wave and a really cute bashful smile. This initial joviality quickly disappeared, however, when the pair of them put two and two together and realised what had happened. It was Ebenezer Dark who spoke first:

'I do believe that we're dead,' he glumly announced in his best solicitor's voice. 'And I do believe that you are culpable!'

'I do believe that you're correct,' said Minnie Driver, in her best solicitor's voice. 'In that we are both dead. However, I do not agree that it is my fault. After all, you were asleep at the wheel.'

'Agreed,' agreed Mr. Dark, 'In that I was asleep at the wheel. However, not only were you asleep at the wheel but you were also driving down the motorway on the wrong side of the road.'

Minnie Driver pondered this for a moment and watched as an ambulance duly appeared at the blood splattered scene. 'I cannot fault the validity of your argument,' she conceded finally. 'For this reason I reluctantly accept culpability and I am willing to make a frankly insulting offer of damages.'

It was at this moment that another voice entered the fray. It was deep, and booming and masterful. LIKE THIS. Except in a really chunky font with better kerning and thunder and lightning coming from the top of the 'H'.

'I am God,' the voice bellowed in a general tone that was a bit like that angry T. Rex in Jurassic Park when that stupid kid shone his torch in its eyes. 'I created everything in six days and then took a day off for a break and I happened to be watching this stretch of the motorway when you crashed.'

Ebenezer Dark looked a little concerned. So did Minnie Driver, only more so.

'This is what happens when you die…' continued God, who, I should explain, looked quite a lot like an old man with a long white beard. He could easily have earned a little extra money in December by posing as Father Christmas, except that he wasn't wearing a red costume; in fact, he didn't seem to be wearing anything at all. (Which sort of begs the question that if you're God and all powerful and omnipotent and all that, why would you make yourself look like a doddering old geriatric without any clothes on instead of, say, Brad Pitt or David Beckham in a really smart suit?) '…You float out of your bodies and I come to collect you so that I can decide whether you go upstairs or downstairs…'

At this point another figure floated into view. He had red skin and horns and hooves like a red skinned hoofed horny goat. He was carrying a large gardening fork. He jovially waved over at the two recently deceased solicitors. He seemed quite friendly actually. He smiled a lot and looked a little like Alan Titchmarsh[13] would if he fell into a vat of indelible red paint.

'If you have lived a worthy and honest life you will go upstairs and spend the rest of eternity having a pretty darned good time,' said God. If, however, you have lived a worthless and dishonest life you will go downstairs and spend the rest of eternity sitting on a blow torch in the depths of hell or somewhere equally horrid such as Burnley…'

It was at this point that God thought for a moment. 'Wait a second,' he announced. 'Aren't you both solicitors?'

---

13   Portly red-faced bloke from the telly. Appears on boring gardening programmes and digs things out of the ground quite a lot.

Ebenezer and Minnie shuffled about uncomfortably and looked downwards at their feet.

Suddenly there was a deafening clap of thunder and God shook his beard angrily, if such a thing is possible – although obviously God can do anything. He didn't say a word. All he did was point his finger downwards and shake his head reproachfully, if such a thing is possible.

Without warning the scene went all shimmery and out of focus. A harp could be heard playing a weird ethereal tune like this: 'da… dada… da… da dada'. You had to be there really. Then Ebenezer Dark awoke to find himself lying on a stretcher in an ambulance. 'Calm down,' said the voice of a white-suited doctor named Doctor White. 'You've had a very bad accident and you've been dreaming.'

'Thank God for that,' said Ebenezer.

'Nothing to do with God,' said Doctor White. 'More to do with this country's woefully unappreciated ambulance service.'

'Am I… Am I… badly injured?' groaned Ebenezer.

'Broken ribs, broken scull, perforated scrotum, pierced lung, pierced ears, ruptured spleen, broken neck, triple heart bypass, very bad cold, carpal tunnel syndrome, repetitive strain injury, fractured skull, in-growing toenail… I don't think you've got long, old boy.'

'How long?' asked Mr. Dark.

'Well, put it this way,' said the doctor, 'I wouldn't bother booking a holiday this year…'

'Oh, dear…'

'In actual fact, if you've got any tickets for the theatre this weekend I'd think about putting them on eBay as quick as you can.'

'In that case I simply have to tell you what I said to Johnny

Nothing when he visited me in my office the other day.'

'Well I can't pretend that I'm interested but if it makes you feel any better getting it off your chest then do go ahead,' said Doctor White.

'I'll do it as a series of bullet points if you don't mind,' said Ebenezer Dark.

'Whatever.'

'I told him to:

● Withdraw some money from the bank account.

● Get rid off all the boxes that were cluttering the flat. Put them up for online auction or something. Put them on Gumtree because Gumtree doesn't charge a 10% commission like other online auction sites.

● Hire some cleaners and decorators and get that dung heap of a flat looking ship shape.

● Get some office furniture to put papers and calculators on.

● Hire Bill and Ben the bodyguard men. In fact, don't bother. I'll arrange it for you.

● Lock your parents up in their bedroom to stop them getting up to any more mischief.

● Telephone me when you've done all this so that I could come to see you and discuss how you are going to get all the money back that your thicko mother has squandered.'

'Really… How interesting…' murmured Doctor White, who was absent-mindedly thumbing through the blood-soaked listings guide of the local newspaper.

Ebenezer Dark closed his eyes for a moment and wondered if he was about to die for real this time. He thought about his life. Had it all been worthwhile? Had he done all the things he'd wanted to do when he was a young ambitious spotty nerd or had he wasted it by becoming a boring old solicitor? You'll find that you probably do the same when you're just about to die, particularly if you end up being a boring old solicitor. Either that or you'll post stink bombs through the letter box of anybody who winds you up. Teachers, headmasters and evil ice-cream men are suitable targets.

It was his father's fault. The rotten swine. His father had been so mean and pushy when Ebenezer was a young bookworm reading copies of Solicitor's Weekly. He'd never let him express himself. His father had forced him to become a solicitor. It was the most boring job in the world apart from, perhaps, a check-out girl in a £1 shop that no one ever goes to because it happens to be right next door to a 99p shop. Now that he was on the verge of death, Ebenezer Dark wanted to tell the whole world about the secret ambition that he had harboured deep inside him for all of his life.

With as much energy as a dying man can muster, Mr. Dark opened his mouth and spat out some words with all his might: 'I want to be a girl!' he cried, feeling truly liberated for the first time in his life. 'I want to be a girl! I want to wear dresses and make-up and go to pretty handbag shops!'

Ebenezer Dark was suddenly aware of another voice speaking to him. 'Mr. Dark,' it said, 'Are you OK? Wake up! Wake up!'

Without warning the scene went all shimmery and out of focus for the second time and Mr. Dark opened his eyes to find himself slumped at the desk in Johnny's little room in the council flat. Johnny was sitting in a chair opposite looking at him strangely. Bill and Ben were standing behind Johnny staring at him with their mouths wide open.

'Hmmm… Sorry about that,' said Mr. Dark. 'I must have drifted off for a moment or two… I was having a dream about having a dream… Happens all the time, y'know.'

'But Mr. Dark, we're supposed to be thinking of ways of earning back the money that my mum has spent,' said Johnny.

'Hmm… That's right…' said Mr. Dark. 'Now where were we?'

Chapter 23 – Plan #2

It had been more than eight months since Uncle Marley's funeral. This is how long it had taken Felicity MacKenzie to spend almost half a million pounds of her son's inheritance. And really, apart from a couple of cars that Billy MacKenzie had bought – even though he couldn't drive – a number of fur coats and various gadgets that were mostly useless, there wasn't a lot to show for it.

Parents, I should tell you, are even worse at handling money than you are. They like to pretend that they're all grown up and responsible but they really can't stop themselves from frittering away the green stuff. Even though they're forever nagging you to save up your pocket money what's the first thing they do on payday? They go out and buy things for themselves. That's what they do and that's what they've always done. And there's no way you can stop them.

Keep an eye out next time it's the last day of the month. If you look closely at your mum and dad when they get home from work you'll be sure to notice that they will be guiltily carrying several packages under their arms. If you ask what they are they'll pretend that they're carrying nothing at all special and head straight for their bedroom. They will be very vague with their answers. They'll say something like: 'Oh, this? It's nothing… Just something I picked up in the post…' Or: 'What package, darling? I don't see any package…'

If you can manage to sneak a camera into their bedroom to record what they're doing you'll then see your mother foaming at the mouth like an alley cat with rabies as she unwraps a new coat or a new handbag or a new dress that cost an absolute fortune. Or you'll see your father's eyes bulging like golfballs as he tears open a new hard disk or computer keyboard or MP3 player, which he will then put in a drawer somewhere and forget all about.

In other words, they're just as bad with money as you are. Even worse in fact. And what I'm trying to say is this: even though Mrs. MacKenzie had quite obviously behaved appallingly by stealing Johnny's cash card and using it to buy thousands of useless rubbishy things that are no good to anybody, don't for a moment imagine that your parents would behave any differently if it happened to you. They might do it in a nicer way but you can be sure that within a few short months your house will be straining under the weight of all the new things that they have bought.

Which brings us back to Johnny:

In under four months it would be a year since everyone had sat in that church watching the video recording of Uncle Marley and listening to him set Johnny his task. This meant that Johnny had very little time left to somehow find a way to get back all the money that his mother had spent. If he could do this he would be able to return to the church and claim ten times the original amount.

This is what Johnny was thinking about as he sat trying to come up with money-making schemes in his bedroom with Ebenezer Dark and Bill and Ben.

It had become apparent to all that money was an incredibly easy thing to get rid of. It was also an incredibly hard thing to get hold of. As everyone saw it, Johnny had a number of options. These included:

1. Get a job

This was an obvious idea but it was fairly flawed because Johnny was not yet old enough to get a job. And unless Johnny managed to get a job as something like the president of Microsoft it was pretty unlikely that he would earn anything close to what what he needed to, which was in the region of £125,000 per month. Not even your headmaster earns that much.

2. Open a sports shop

This was Ben's idea. He thought it would be great if Johnny spent some of the remaining £510,000 on an shop that sold exercise gear. Bill thought that this was not as silly an idea as you might imagine. Given that the vast majority of people in this country have bellies that are bigger than Buddha's and Christopher Biggins' put together Ben thought there would be a great demand for exercise gear.

3. Open a burger bar

Bill went the other way. Since most people in this country have bellies that are bigger than Buddah's and Christopher Biggins' put together, he thought it might be an even better idea to start a burger bar to help make those bellies even bigger.

4. Start a bank

What other business in the world asks people to give them all their money for free and then charges them a fee to withdraw little bits of it every now and again? That, in Johnny's opinion, was all that banks did. Mr. Dark, who knew a lot more about these things than Johnny, thought about this for some time but could not find a good reason to disagree. However, the problem once again was that Johnny was simply too young to be allowed to do this.

5. Rob a bank

Once again Bill and Ben were more than happy to try this. Johnny and Mr. Dark thought it best if they put this idea on the back burner. (Don't rob banks, kids!)

6. Play the stock market

Uncle Marley had actually planted this idea in Johnny's mind. Remember the funeral? When he said: 'Or you could try your hand at the stock market. That's an easy way to win – and lose – a fortune.'

I don't know if you have ever tried playing the stock market with your dinner money? Try it tomorrow for a bit of fun. What it basically entails is gambling on how much something is going to cost in a year or so's time. It's a bit like saying: 'I bet £5 that gobstoppers will cost 50p each next term.' If you're right you get a lot more money back. If you're wrong you lose all your money and get stoned to death by an avalanche of angry gobstopper investors.

Everyone in the room agreed that this was a risky strategy. However, Bill and Ben were willing to give it a go.

7. Go to Las Vegas

Everyone was a little bit keen on this idea. They would all fly to Las Vegas and go to a casino and try to win back the money by playing Blackjack or Five-Card Stud. Bill and Ben were so excited about doing this that they even got as far as looking at airport departure times. However, when it was discovered that nobody in the room actually knew what Blackjack or Five-Card Stud was the idea was reluctantly dropped.

8. Win the lottery

It was Johnny who suggested that they withdraw all the cash they had left and purchase 500,000 or so lottery tickets. 'Surely one of the would be a winner?' he said. However, the idea was quickly abandoned when Mr. Dark explained that one had more chance of winning the lottery than one had of being struck by lightning. The idea was very quickly dumped, despite the flat unexpectedly being struck by lightning three times that after-noon during a freak thunderstorm that appeared from nowhere and disappeared just as suddenly.

9. Invent something amazing

On face value this seemed like one of the better ideas. All you had do was think of something that nobody had ever thought of and you could then make lots and lots of money out of it.

The group sat and thought for a long, long time. Finally they came up with a list of suggestions. Unfortunately, all of them were rejected because:

- The orbital satellite had been around forever.
- The concept of a rocket had already taken flight.
- The sombrero was old hat.
- The printing press was yesterday's news.
- The sugar-powered internal combustion engine was a non-starter.
- The waste disposal unit was simply a rubbish idea.
- The notion of carpets made of sandpaper was for the birds (although it gave Ben a trill).
- The everlasting handkerchief was not to be sneezed at.
- A self-making dough machine was the last thing anyone kneaded.
- The idea for an egg-shaped football was quickly kicked into touch.
- Invisible stain remover was a washout.
- The disposable clock was a waste of time.
- The idea for a giant chicken was a real turkey.
- The idea for a legless bird was just a lame duck.

'Let's face it,' said Mr. Dark, after they had all been sitting together in the room for more than a day. 'We can't think of a single good idea.'

'I'm out,' said Bill.

'We started badly and went downhill from there,' added Ben.

'I'm not wasting my children's inheritance on this,' agreed Johnny.

Chapter 24 – Tramp

Another month rushed by. And that was that – or so it seemed. No matter how much they wracked their brains neither Johnny nor the three grown-ups could think of any way of getting back the money that Felicity MacKenzie had squandered. She had proven to be far more successful at spending money than they were at earning it.

Johnny had no choice but to face up to the fact that he would never be able to complete Uncle Marley's task. He felt a failure, which was a little unfortunate really. Because I think you'll agree that you couldn't blame Johnny for wasting all that money. It wasn't his fault.

But things were far from over. There were a number of questions that needed to be answered. Firstly, what was to be done with his parents? It was certainly tempting but it wasn't really practical to keep them locked away forever. And if and when

Johnny finally did set them free, he was reasonably sure that they were going to be far from happy.

There was also the question of Bill and Ben. Johnny really liked having them around. In fact, a large part of him wished that he could permanently swap them for his parents. Naturally, one of the two would have to wear his mother's clothing and speak in a high-pitched voice. Johnny wasn't entirely sure if that would work, although he could think of one or two teachers at school that seemed to resemble men dressed as women and they got away with it. I'm sure you can, too. Deep down, however, Johnny knew that sooner or later he would have to let them leave.

At least Johnny could console himself that he still had half of Uncle Marley's money left. £1/2 million was an awful lot of money by anyone's standards. He was still the richest schoolboy that he knew. If Johnny was careful and didn't go crazy he was sure that he could make the money last for a very, very long time. As long as he could keep his mother's hands off the cash card, life could be made so much better for the whole family.

They could buy a nice little house somewhere. They could invest the money and live off the interest. They could move into the country and become gardeners or something. Whatever the case, life was sure to be a far more pleasant experience than the one that Johnny used to live.

However, as he pondered what to do with his inheritance life still had to go on. For this reason Johnny simply carried on doing the things he always did. He ate breakfast. He did his homework at night. He went to school like he always had done. The only real difference is that he didn't look quite so scruffy – Johnny had allowed himself to spend a little money on a set of new clothing. In addition to this, very few people at school now called him Johnny Nothing. He was back to being plain old

Johnny MacKenzie. And he liked it.

But things were about to change.

It so happened that Johnny was walking to school one morning when he was approached by a smelly old tramp who asked him for money. Being a kind and generous person by nature, Johnny reached into his pocket and gave him everything it contained. There was about £1.50 – nothing to a boy who was as rich as Johnny.

When school was over that day Johnny was surprised to see that the wretched hobo was still waiting for him outside the school. Standing beside him was an ugly old hag. Although scruffy and dressed in vile, rancid rags, the pair made quite a nice couple actually. Not handsome or anything like that. Repulsive and rank and flea infested. A sort of vagrant version of Will and Kate. Once again the revolting fellow asked for money and once again Johnny obligingly dipped into his pocket. This time, however, it was empty.

'Sorry about that,' explained Johnny. 'But if you come back tomorrow I'll make sure that I've got something to give you.' The pair of beggars grumbled to themselves in the trampy sort of way that old tramps always do but agreed they would return.

Sure enough, when Johnny arrived at school the next day the unwholesome, rotten-faced, nicotine stained duo were again waiting for him. Johnny gave them each £5. About a year's wages for an upwardly mobile lazy old tramp. They stared at the money in their poo stained hands and said a grudging thank you that sounded nothing like a thank you.

This is the things about tramps – however much you give them they never actually look very pleased about it. I can't think why. If you don't believe me try giving some money to a dirty old dodderer wrapped up in old newspapers in the street. You can take the money back off him once you've confirmed that what I'm saying is definitely the truth. He probably won't mind.

When Johnny got out of school later that day there were now four stinky old tramps loitering at the gates. He had been half expecting to see the original gruesome couple waiting for him, but he was a little surprised to see that two extra lice-infested tramps had joined them. Once again he handed out some money and went on his way without receiving much in the way of a thank-you for his troubles.

When he arrived at the school gates the next day it was apparent that things were beginning to get out of hand. Outside the school he counted a total of eleven loathsome old vagrants. That was a whole football team of useless tramps. All of them were dressed in really bad charity shop rags. They looked a bit like a really rubbish team from the Conference League.

Johnny did some calculations on his calculator. If he gave each of these vile, smelly people a couple of quid a day it could easily run into hundreds of pounds every week. He decided that he'd better not give them any more. However, as luck would have it just at that moment he happened to look down at his feet. A week or so ago he had bought himself a shiny new pair of trainers. It was the first brand new pair of trainers that he had ever owned.

He looked at the shoes, remembering that not so long ago he had been wearing his father's foot-me-downs. And he looked at his clothes, which were also new. He remembered that not so long ago he, too, had been wearing charity shop rejects.

Although the idea was that Johnny was supposed to be finding a way to recoup the money that his parents had squandered he couldn't help himself. Once again he reached into his pockets and gave away all the money that he was carrying. He even went hungry at lunch time because of this.

When he got out of school that afternoon Johnny could not believe what he saw. There were now about fifty degenerate old street walkers waiting for him. In addition to this there were a number of pregnant women smoking cigarettes and pushing prams full of screeching infants that smelled of baby wee. When the group saw him they all held out their hands and asked for money. Johnny didn't really want to but he couldn't stop himself.

'Listen,' he said. 'I don't have a lot of money on me but if you follow me I'll withdraw some from the cash point.'

Just like his mother had before him, Johnny now carried the cash card around him at all times. He hadn't gone all psycho and started calling it '**MY PRECIOUS**' or anything. It had been so difficult for him to prise it out of the hands of Mrs. MacKenzie that he just didn't want to risk losing it. And now he pushed the cash card into a nearby cash point and handed out the notes that spilled from it.

Within seconds, hundreds of hands had engulfed him and all the cash he had withdrawn was gone.

'Please,' he said. 'I can't do this every day. Just this once. You'll have to go somewhere else tomorrow.'

However, it was clear that although the crowd wanted his money they were not prepared to accept his advice. When he awoke the next morning Johnny heard murmurings outside the door of the council flat. When he looked out of the window he could see a crowd of about three hundred people waiting on the landing and on the pavement outside the building. Some of them were vile, grime-encrusted beggars, and there were more pregnant women with cigarettes and buggies. There also a few people among the group in fairly smart looking suits.

Johnny opened a window and poked his head out. 'Erm… Can I help you?' he asked nervously.

There was a short silence and then one of the throng replied: 'Sorry… But do you have a spare 20p?'

Then the crowd began to chant his name. 'Johnny!' Johnny!' they shouted.

'Stop it,' said Johnny, although his voice could not be heard above the din.

'Johnny! Johnny! We want Johnny Nothing!'

'Who's there?' the voice of Felicity MacKenzie managed to escape from the locked up bedroom upstairs. She had been awoken from the dream about pork scratchings that she was having in Chapter 21. She was confused and slightly annoyed.

'Its… Erm… Some people.'

'What do they want?'

'They… Erm… Want some money.'

'Tell 'em to go away…' cried Mrs. MacKenzie. 'Lazy dossers!'

He didn't really want to but Johnny got dressed and went down to the same cash machine as yesterday. Once again he withdrew some money and distributed it among the pursuing crowd.

This pattern continued for another week or two. Wherever Johnny went he was followed by hundreds of people. The majority were genuinely needy but there was always a small number of people who were out to get as much as they possibly could from the young boy who gave out free money.

Call it weakness. Call it stupidity. Call it genuine kindness if you like. But Johnny simply didn't have it in him to say no to any of them.

One morning Ebenezer Dark came to visit him. After pushing his way through the crowd of beggars and leeches that were hanging around Johnny's front door he said:

'Johnny! What have you been doing? I've just checked your bank account and you're spending money at a **RIDICULOUS** rate. You're spending it even faster than your mother did!'

Johnny looked guiltily at Mr. Dark and shrugged his shoulders. 'I'm sorry,' he said. 'But all these people have no money. They're really starving.'

'My dear boy,' said Mr. Dark. 'You really can't go on like this. If you carry on spending your money at this rate it'll be you who's outside begging.'

'I know,' said Johnny. 'But I've got to give them something.'

Mr. Dark gave Johnny something – a firm talking to. He demanded that Johnny give him the cash card so that he could put a halt to the spending. But Johnny had fought so long and hard to get it back from his mum he was unwilling to surrender it.

'Listen, Johnny,' said Mr. Dark. 'If you're dead set on giving your money away let's do it properly. Why don't you let me set up a proper charity so that the money is distributed fairly. It's also a good way of avoiding paying tax, don't you know?'

'No thank you,' replied Johnny. 'There's no need to make it official. I can handle it myself.'

But next day letters started to arrive. Hundreds and hundreds of letters from people with heartbreakingly tragic tales to tell. Hundreds of people begging him for money.

Here's a typical example:

DEAR JOHNNY,

I hope you don't mind me writing to you but my mother and father have just died in a plane crash. This means that me and my poor baby sister who suffers from very bad psoriasis will have to go to into a foster home where they are sure to beat us and force us to work as chimney sweeps and feed us gruel and stuff.

Please can you help us by sending us some money so that we won't be horse whipped every Sunday and have our lives completely ruined.

You don't have to send us that much. Just enough to get us through private school.

Yours sincerely,
B JOHNSON

PS Please, please, please help us.
PPS We accept all major credit cards or you can transfer money to our PayPal account at: bjohnson.gov.com
Johnny became the boy who couldn't say no. If anybody asked him for money he simply gave it to them. If they wrote to him begging for money he could not stop himself from replying with letters stuffed with cash.

Bill and Ben and Mr. Dark tried to call a halt to his generosity but Johnny would not listen. His mother and father, still safely locked away in their bedroom, yelled through the door for him to stop. But he would not.

For most of his life he had been the poorest boy in school. He had gotten used to a life without money. And now that he was the richest boy in school Johnny realised that it meant nothing to him. Money was just crinkled up pieces of paper or shards of moulded metal. If he could help another person by giving away some of this paper and metal why would he not do so?

What a div, thought his mother.

Chapter 25 – Famous #1

Another couple of weeks went by and the number of people that were gathered outside Johnny Nothing's council flat grew and grew and grew. And never once did Johnny turn away any poor person who asked him for money. He also sent money to nearly all of the people who wrote letters to him. Instead of being his bodyguards Bill and Ben spent most of their time opening letters for Johnny. He even sent a couple of sackfuls of letters to his parents to open in their room upstairs.

Although they moaned a lot about it, his parents eventually agreed to help him with opening and answering the letters. This was not because they had suddenly become possessed by the spirt of Mother Theresa or Noel Edmonds. It was simply because they were **BORED**. In fact, they were so **BORED** locked away in their bedroom that they were crawling up the walls. Bill and Ben surveyed the damage to the walls that had been caused by this and told them to stop doing it and open letters instead.

One morning there was a knock on the front door. Let me rephrase that: every morning there was a knock on the front door. Let me rephrase that: every five seconds or so there was a knock on the front door. It was really annoying actually, Johnny couldn't get a moment's peace from people knocking on his door and asking for money.

On this occasion, however, it wasn't somebody asking for money. It was far worse than that. It was a newspaper reporter.

Johnny could see instantly that it was a newspaper reporter because the fellow in question was wearing a badge on his lapel that read: 'Newspaper reporter'. He could also tell that it was a newspaper reporter because the bloke had a really shifty expression on his face and held a notebook in his hand. He looked like the sort of person who would sell his mother to white slave traders for a packet of crisps and can of Coke.

'You the kid who's giving away money?' the man enquired.

"Erm… Yes… I suppose so,' replied Johnny suspiciously.

'Well my name's Terry Pryor and I'm from the Gazette,' he continued. 'I've come to do a story on the kid who's giving away money. That you? What's your name?'

'Johnny MacKenzie… But everyone calls me Johnny Nothing.'

Terry Pryor wrote this down. 'Why's that?' he asked.

'Why's what?'

'Why'd they call you Johnny Nothing when you've obviously not got nothing?'

'Cos I used to have nothing and now I've got something.'

Terry Pryor wrote this down, too. 'Where'd you get this something from?'

'From my Uncle Marley.'

'I see…' said Terry Pryor. 'And how do I get in touch with this Uncle Marley?'

'You can't.'

'No need to be rude, kid. I'm just doing my job…'

'I mean you can't cos he's dead.'

Terry Pryor wrote this down. 'I don't get this,' he said. 'How can this dead Uncle Marley be giving you something when he'd dead? He a ghost or something?'

'No. He left me some money in his will.'

'Aww… Gotcha…' said Terry Pryor. 'And how much'd he leave you?'

'He left me a million pounds,' replied Johnny.

"Blimey! A million quid…' Exclaimed Terry Pryor. 'You're rich kid!'

'Not really. My mum spent half of it and I've given most of the rest away to these people,' said Johnny, pointing at the congregation of tramps, social misfits, runaways, single mothers and ex-financial advisors that were a permanent fixture outside his door.

'Givin' it away! Are you mad?' exclaimed Terry Pryor.

Johnny shrugged guiltily. 'My mum and dad think so and so does Mr. Dark,' he said.

But Terry Pryor's eyes were widening and nostrils were distending. 'Hold on a minute…' he said excitedly, smelling a story. 'You ain't mad kid… You're a hero.'

'What?' said Johnny.

'I can just see the headline: "**HERO SCHOOLBOY GIVES AWAY MILLIONS!**"'

The journalist stayed another half-an-hour and asked Johnny lots of stupid questions. He wrote down all of Johnny's answers in his notebook in a kind of scribble that nobody – not even Terry Pryor – could read.

Finally, he put the notebook away and waved goodbye. 'Take a look at tomorrow's paper, kid,' he said.

ISLINGTON GAZETTE

04 May 2013

TRAMPS A MILLION!

By Terrance 'Weasel' Pryor

Schoolboy idiot Johnny Nothing is giving away all his money. That's right. If you head over to his council flat in North London he's giving away everything he's got.

Nothing, 10, inherited the fortune from the late eccentric commodities millionaire Jacob Marley. But instead of holding on to it like most sensible people would do, he's been giving his dosh away to the homeless and underprivileged.

Said Nothing yesterday: 'I don't really care about money so I'm giving it all away. Please come round to my council flat and claim your share before I run out of it.'

Above the story was a picture of Johnny that had obviously been taken when he was on the way to school. Johnny read the story and his mouth hung open.

And then he said the mantra that anybody who has every had their name in a newspaper will always say: 'I never said that!' he exclaimed.

Chapter 26 – Viral

O n the same day that the newspaper story was published in the local paper a BBC film crew pulled up outside the MacKenzie's council flat. It was accompanied by a number of reporters from other newspapers and magazines as well as a second film crew – this one from Belgium.

They were all keen to watch and record as Johnny Nothing continued to give away his money to the poor, needy and ex-ploited. It was a becoming a big story.

Several of the journalists interviewed Johnny. Some inter-viewed Bill and Ben, who explained that they were there to 'look after Johnny and his money'. Some interviewed Mr. Dark, who didn't say very much but walked around looking worried and muttering under his breath about handbags or something.

Some asked about Johnny's parents. They were told that Fe-licity and Billy were 'visiting some relatives'. Felicity MacKenzie, however, saw all this unexpected attention as an ideal means of escaping. Once, when Johnny was being interviewed by Channel 4, his mother began frantically tapping on the floor of the bedroom while her husband hammered on the door.

'Were getting a little interference,' said a Channel 4 sound technician.

'We'll sort it out,' announced Bill and Ben. 'We got some very noisy neighbours.'

With that the musclebound twins went upstairs and quickly bound and gagged Johnny's parents.

'Sorry about this,' said Bill, although he wasn't sorry at all. 'But we can't have you ruining things can we?'

In the following days more stories appeared in the newspapers. And with each story that was published more people came to watch as Johnny Nothing gave away his money it seemed to anybody who asked.

Footage of Johnny appeared on the breakfast shows of all the main TV channels and as his celebrity grew, even more people gathered around the MacKenzie's council flat.

Finally, someone uploaded footage of Johnny to YouTube and it instantly went viral. Millions of people from all over the world stopped watching Gangnam Style and videos of babies singing and tuned in instead to look at the youngster from North London who was giving away his fortune. Johnny couldn't dance and he couldn't sing but, boy, was he good at handing out money.

He was too good: Day after day the money in Johnny's bank account continued to dwindle.

'Why are you doing this?' asked Mr. Dark one morning.

'I don't know,' replied Johnny. 'It just seems unfair that I've got all this money when people around are starving and have nowhere to live.'

'That's all very laudable,' said Mr. Dark. 'But what about Mr. Marley's task? Have you forgotten all about it?'

In truth Johnny had forgotten all about the task that his late uncle had set him. When they had been unable to come up with a money making idea that could possibly get back all the cash that his mother had spent, Johnny had almost given up on the idea. It seemed impossible to earn back almost £1/2 million in less than four months. And now there was only a month to go and the idea was simply ludicrous.

'I don't think we're going to be able to do Uncle Marley's task,' admitted Johnny. 'I don't really think that it was ever possible.'

Mr. Dark shook his head sadly. 'What a pity,' he said. 'I really thought that you would be able to achieve it.'

But while Ebenezer Dark could not hide his disappointment for Johnny, the rest of the world simply could not stop looking at him. It was like Johnny Nothing was a rock star. Wherever he went people called out his name. If they weren't asking for money they were asking for his autograph. He was the boy who gave away money. He was on his way to becoming one of the most famous people in the country.

Every day he appeared on the front pages of the national newspapers. Sometimes he was even in the sports pages and sometimes he was in the gossip pages. But he was more or less oblivious to his fame. He simply carried on as normal. That's if you can call living-with-twin-Neanderthal-bodyguards-while-keeping-your-parents-looked-away-in-their-bedroom-while-handing-out-money-to-anyone-who-asks-for-it normal.

One afternoon Johnny left school for the day to find a bigger crowd than ever waiting for him outside. Like a group of football supporters they chanted his name as he walked along the street. Cameras flashed as he made his daily trip to the cash point.

Because the crowd was so large today Johnny would have to withdraw even more money than usual.

He put the cash card into the slot and keyed in his number. He waited for a moment while the machine went about its business. There was a brief delay. And then Johnny stepped backwards and gasped. As the crowd looked on the blood drained from his face and he went pale with shock.

On the black screen of the cashpoint were two words in bright green letters:

INSUFFICIENT FUNDS

Johnny frowned and checked that he had not made a mistake. He took the card out of the machine and again tried to withdraw cash.

Once more the two words gleamed up at him.

Johnny let the information sink in. This had to be some sort of mistake. A bank error.

He put the card in the machine a third time. He held his breath and waited. Once again it refused to give him any more money.

Johnny covered his face with hands and felt himself go faint. Was this really it? Was there really nothing left of the money that his uncle had left him? Johnny had not looked at a bank statement for some time. In truth he had been a little scared of doing so. Johnny had stopped keeping a tally of what he was spending. Surely it can't all have gone?

Johnny looked around in horror at the crowd of people surrounding him. They could hardly hear him as he whispered:

'I'm very sorry, but I have no more money to give you.'

'What did he say?' asked a voice in the crowd.

'He said he wants some honey…' said another.

Johnny repeated himself, louder this time. 'I'm very sorry,' he called. 'But there's no money left.'

There was a murmur of discontentment from the crowd. 'He says there's no more money!' someone exclaimed.

'No more money!' cried another. 'What's he mean there's no more money?!'

'He's lying!' said another voice.

Johnny shook his head as the crowd grew restless. 'It's true!' he cried. 'I've got nothing left to give you!'

'Boohhh!' exclaimed several members of the crowd.

'It's all gone!' yelled Johnny.

Suddenly the crowd began to boo in earnest. The sound rose in a great crescendo and drowned out the noises of traffic and any passing light aircraft.

'Booh! Booh! Johnny Nothing! Booh!' chanted the crowd, some even beginning to throw things in Johnny's direction.

Johnny broke into a trot and then a sprint as a shower of tin cans, empty cigarette cartons, old rolled up newspapers and pieces of indeterminate rubbish began to rain down on him. He ran as fast as he could along the road that led to the council flat. Pushing his way through the crowds that were waiting outside his home he fled in fear as news of what had happened reached them. With the crowd raging he managed to open his front door. Discarded bottles, stones and old used nappies struck the door as he closed it.

The sounds of shouting and booing were deafening as Johnny made his way into his bedroom and slammed the door shut. There he lay on his bed and covered his ears with his hands as a riot ensued on the balcony outside.

The money was gone. It was all gone.

Chapter 27 – Failure

Johnny woke up the next morning still in his school clothing. For a moment he forgot all about the events of yesterday: The money running out. The near riot that ensued outside the council flat. He forgot about the police turning up in riot gear to disperse the crowd. The helicopters circling the estate. And the terrible feeling in the pit of his stomach at the grim realisation that all of Uncle Marley's inheritance was gone for good.

And then everything came slowly back to him and Johnny felt a terrible failure. How was it possible to spend a million pounds in less than a year? What was he going to tell Mr. Dark? Bill and Ben? His father? His mother? How could have been so stupid as to give away all that money to total strangers. What a fool he was.

It was then that he noticed something.

He should have noticed it at once but he had been too busy

thinking. He had become so used to the sound of the crowd outside the flat, to the incessant tapping on the front door, to the sound of camera shutters whirring away that now that they were no longer there he did not notice the silence.

Silence.

The sound of complete and utter silence.

Johnny went into the kitchen to find Bill and Ben sitting at the kitchen table grimly having a cup of tea. They did not speak when they saw him. They simply nodded sadly. The look on both their faces was a combination of sorrow and guilt: they were sorry that Johnny had somehow managed to lose all his money. And they felt guilty because they been hired to protect him and that money – something they had very obviously failed to do.

Later that morning Ebenezer Dark appeared. He wore the same expression as the twin bodyguards. 'I'm so sorry, Johnny,' he said. 'I tried to warn you that the money wouldn't last forever…'

'It's all right Mr. Dark,' said Johnny. 'It's nobody else's fault but my own.'

Mr. Dark shook his head and looked down at his feet. 'You do realise, of course, that things must now change?' he said.

Johnny looked at him.

'Now that you have no more money you simply cannot afford to keep Bill and Ben here.'

Johnny turned to regard the twins.

'Sorry kid,' said Bill. 'We'd really like to stay here but we have a living to earn, you know.'

'He's right,' agreed Ben. 'We'd love to stay and help you out but we can't not do it for nothing.'

'This also unfortunately means that Mr. and Mrs. Mackenzie

must be allowed to leave their bedroom,' continued Mr. Dark. 'We put them there to keep them away from the money. Now that it's gone…'

'Don't worry. I knew I couldn't keep them there forever,' said Johnny.

'We could give them a good kicking if you like,' said Bill.

'On the house… Our present… No charge…' said Ben.

'That's all right,' smiled Johnny weakly. 'They are my parents in spite of everything.'

Ebenezer Dark put a consoling arm around Johnny's shoulders. 'I'm afraid that life will very much have to return to what it was before…'

'I know…' said Johnny.

'I really thought that you'd do it,' said Mr. Dark. 'I really wanted to be back in that church when you arrived with more than a million and claimed your reward.'

'Me too,' said Johnny.

'Us three and four,' chorused Bill and Ben.

'I suppose you can console yourself that the money that you had went to, well – mostly – worthy causes,' said Mr. Dark.

Bill and Ben slowly began packing up their belongings. They didn't have much. Just a few knuckle dusters, the taser and a few back issues of Practical Bodyguard. Then they went upstairs to release Johnny's parents.

There was a lot of shouting from above as Bill and Ben gave Johnny's mum and dad a severe talking to. Johnny couldn't hear most of what was said but he did catch the end of one of Ben's sentences: '…and if we ever hear that you're treating the kid bad we'll be paying you a visit…'

Johnny's parents came down to the kitchen, squinting into the light. Both had lost a lot of weight and both looked considerably healthier than they had done before their enforced imprisonment. Felicity MacKenzie had a curious expression on her face as she regarded her son.

'Hello mum,' said Johnny softly.

'All gone has it?' said Mrs. MacKenzie.

'I'm sorry…' said Johnny.

'You will be you little…'

Before she could finish her words Bill cut in: 'Enough,' he said. 'Remember what I said.'

Mrs. MacKenzie looked a little like a pet dog after it has had a telling off. Clutching her husband's hand she moved shakily off to the living room.

'I guess this is goodbye then, kid,' said Bill.

'Yeah,' said Ben. ''Fraid it's tah-tah time…'

The two giants reached down and gently placed their gigantic arms around the young boy. Johnny had to try hard to stop himself from crying. However, when the embrace was over he could feel tears running down his cheek. They were not his own.

His farewell to Mr. Dark was rather more formal. The older man took his hand in both of his and gave it a hearty shake. 'Goodbye, my boy,' he said slowly. 'Once again I'm sorry about how it all turned out. Do feel free to give me a call if you should ever need any advice.'

And with that the two giant bodyguards and the rather less gigantic solicitor exited the MacKenzie flat. Johnny was left alone with his two parents for the first time in months. It was as it always had been.

And as it always had been, as soon as they were alone Felicity MacKenzie marched into the kitchen with a fiery expression on her face. She was no longer looking like a pet dog after a telling off. She was a wild animal (a bit like at the opening of chapter 18). Two months of anger and frustration at being locked away had been stored up. And now she was ready to let fly with all that anger.

'You stupid little freak!' she yelled. 'How dare you steal my **PRECIOUS**. How dare you lock me away in my own bedroom! How dare you spend all MY money.'

But Johnny was no longer as terrified of his mother as he once was. 'It wasn't your money,' he replied with real steel in his voice. 'It was my money to do with what I wanted.'

This was probably the first time that Johnny had ever really stood up to his mother in his whole life. And like most bullies when they are confronted by their victims, Mrs. MacKenzie was a little freaked out by this new development. She stopped her shouting and stared her son right in the eyes.

A staring match ensued just like you might have occasionally in the school playground. With Johnny refusing to look away from his mother. And Mrs. MacKenzie refusing to look away from Johnny. Nobody blinked because blinking was not allowed. Felicity MacKenzie's eyes began to water. Johnny's eyes began to water.

The tension grew until after what seemed an eternity but in fact was more like 45 seconds, Mrs. MacKenzie finally looked away. Johnny had won.

'Your money? Yes, and just look what you did with it!' said Mrs. MacKenzie in a gentler voice. 'You've given it all away to a load of losers!! You complete imbecile!'

'I don't care,' said Johnny. 'I'd rather have given it to people who needed it than watch you waste it on nothing.'

His mother fell silent for a moment. Johnny wasn't sure what she was going to do next. Then she seemed to calm down a little. An evil smile spread over her face and she spoke:

'Yes… **NOTHING**,' she said. '**NOTHING**'s the word isn't it? You given everything away and now we have **NOTHING**. I have **NOTHING**. Billy has **NOTHING**. And you have **NOTHING**. Nothing! Nothing Nothing! You're **JOHNNY NOTHING**!!'

And with that Felicity MacKenzie began to giggle. It was no normal giggle. It was the giggle of a madwoman. It was the giggle of one of those witches in the opening scene of Macbeth or Sharon Osborne when she sends dog poo through the post to people who annoy her. Felicity MacKenzie laughed. And she laughed. And she laughed. And she laughed until she could laugh no more.

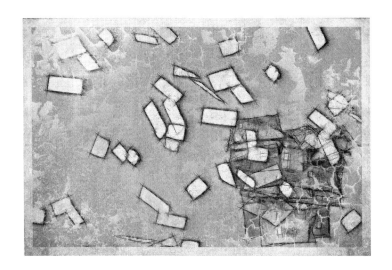

Chapter 28 – Letters

And so life returned to normal.

Johnny went to school five days a week and his brief celebrity was slowly forgotten about. There were no more groups of beggars and tramps waiting for Johnny outside the school gates. There were no more headlines in the newspapers. The YouTube videos were played even less than Jordan's Eurovision Song Contest entry. There were no more items on the television about the boy who gave away money.

Johnny MacKenzie was once more Johnny Nothing. And a part of him was secretly pleased about this.

But there had been a few subtle changes. For one thing, Mrs. MacKenzie was just a little bit nicer to him. Not too much, mind you, because a woman with a leopard skin coat cannot change her spots. But just a little bit nicer. She no longer shouted at him quite so much. She no longer called him names quite so much. And although she would never get over the fact that she was no longer stinking rich, even she was a little bit pleased that everything had gotten back to what it was before Uncle Marley's funeral.

For his part Billy MacKenzie was also relieved that normality had returned. Although he had never complained, he hadn't liked like the posh hotels and the posh holidays. And he hadn't liked the posh meals that his wife had forced him to eat. He liked the simple life. He was a pie and chips man. Which was just as well because most of the time that was all the family could afford to eat.

The anniversary of Uncle Marley's funeral was only three days away but nobody really noticed. They were too busy ignoring the pile of unpaid bills that grew like a miniature tower block at the foot of the letterbox. Life was as hard as it had always been. Felicity MacKenzie wasted what little money they had on cigarettes and booze. Billy MacKenzie spent what was left at the betting shop. The family were on first name terms with the bailiffs that regularly called around. They were always one step away from financial disaster. And Johnny could look forward to things being this way for a very long time to come.

But once again things were about to change.

One morning Johnny was walking to school when he noticed that someone was following him. He slowed down a little so that he could get a better look at the person. It was Terry Pryor, the reporter who had done the first story about him.

'Hey Johnny can I have a word?' he said.

'What about?' asked Johnny.

'I just wanted to ask a couple of questions,' said Terry Pryor.

'The last time I did that you printed a load of lies about me.'

'Oh… Yes… Sorry about that… It was my editor… They take

what I write and then make it up if it isn't interesting enough… It won't happen this time. I promise.'

Johnny turned away and carried on walking to school, ignoring the reporter.

'Don't be like that,' said Terry. 'I only want to to a little follow-up story… See how you've been getting on since you done all your dosh.'

'I'm perfectly all right, thank-you very much,' said Johnny.

Terry Pryor wrote this down.

'Don't write it down,' exclaimed Johnny. 'I don't want any more stories in the papers about me.'

Terry Pryor wrote this down.

'Stop writing it down!' said Johnny.

'You not having a good time then?'

'What do you mean?'

'Things hard for you now that you're poor again?'

'Things are fine,' said Johnny, continuing to walk away.

Terry Pryor wrote this down.

'How have you been managing without all that money?' asked Terry Pryor.

'We're managing fine thanks.'

Terry Pryor wrote this down.

'Your mum and dad angry that you've blown your wad?'

Johnny stopped. 'Look,' he said. 'Please leave me alone. I just want to get to school and forget about everything that's happened.'

Terry Pryor wrote this down.

'Just one more thing and I'll leave you alone…' said Terry Pryor.

'What?'

'You got any regrets?'

'What do you mean?'

'Regrets. Do you think you should have saved all that money instead of giving it to a load of old wasters?'

'No… At least somebody benefitted from the money. I know I didn't.'

Terry Pryor wrote this down. 'Thanks kid,' he said. 'That's all I need. Have a look at the paper tomorrow…'

ISLINGTON GAZETTE

12 July 2013

SCHOOLBOY LOSER HAS NO REGRETS

By Terrance 'Weasel' Pryor

The boy who gave away all his money to tramps and the unemployed says he would do it all again. Johnny 'Nothing' MacKenzie, 10, told the Gazette that he has 'no regrets' about spending all of his uncle's inheritance and only wishes he had more money to give away.

MacKenzie, who has returned to abject poverty, now has more in common with the tramps he gave his money away to. When we spoke to him last night he was wearing rags and said he had not 'eaten properly for a whole week'.

MacKenzie inherited £1 Million from a rich relative but wasted the whole lot on beggars and losers. If he had kept the money the interest alone would have earned him £200 per day.

When we spoke to his mother, Felicity MacKenzie, 44, she told us: 'The boy's an idiot. He has no idea of the value of money. We could have lived the rest of our lives in luxury but he has to give it away to the dregs of society.'

'It's the boy himself who should be getting donations,' said his father, Billy MacKenzie, 51, 'All those people who he gave money to should be sending him cash! He's a complete wally!'

***

Johnny was not at all surprised when he read the story in the newspaper the next day. He had expected lies to be printed. The same, however, could not be said of his mother and father: 'Bloody cheek,' said Felicity MacKenzie. 'I never said anything of the sort. And they got my age wrong!'

But when Johnny awoke the next morning something unexpected happened. Nestling next to the tower block of bills beneath the letter box were a couple of letters addressed to him. When he opened them to his great surprise a small quantity of coins dropped out on to the carpet. Johnny read the letters – they were from people who had seen the newspaper article. They told him how kind and generous he was and how they wanted to make a little contribution to his 'fund'.

Johnny smiled and put the coins in his pocket.

Later in the afternoon there was a knock on the front door. It was the same film crew from the BBC that had visited previously. They wanted to shoot a short item about what had happened to Johnny Nothing now that he had given all his money away.

'How are you surviving without any money?' asked one of the presenters.

'We're doing OK,' said Johnny. 'My mum and dad get state benefits and people have started sending me this.'

Johnny pointed at the envelopes and the small pile of coins.

'People are sending you money?' said the man from the BBC.

'Well… Not much,' said Johnny.

'Have you started a fund?'

'No. The money just arrived out of the blue.'

A couple of mornings later Johnny was surprised to discover more than a dozen letters addressed to him had arrived through the letter box. Johnny opened the letters and discovered more coins inside. There were even a few notes. Johnny read the letters with interest. Apparently people had seen the item about him on BBC news and decided that they wanted to help. Once again there were more knocks on the door from other newspapers and more film crews. They wanted to film him and interview him.

Johnny Nothing was once again becoming a celebrity.

Later that day a large lorry could be seen pulling into the grounds of the council estate. A team of burly postmen emerged from the lorry carrying hundreds and hundreds of letters and parcels all addressed to Johnny. All of them contained money. Most people had sent loose change to Johnny but some had sent £5 and £10 notes. The packages did not stop arriving. Soon there was nowhere to put all the money they contained.

Johnny had no idea what to do next. Without thinking, he dug out the mobile phone from Uncle Marley's briefcase and rang Ebenezer Dark to tell him what was happening.

'Oh my word!' exclaimed Mr. Dark. 'Hold on and I'll be right over.'

Chapter 29 – Money #2

'One for him… Two for me…' muttered Felicity Mackenzie under her breath. 'One for him… Two for me…'

Mrs. MacKenzie was opening letters and taking out the money they contained. For once in her life she didn't seem to mind doing a little work. It was her kind of job. Along with Billy MacKenzie, Bill and Ben, Mr. Dark and Johnny, she was helping to sort the money out into piles. Letters were arriving all the time. It was almost impossible to keep up with them.

The flat was overwhelmed by piles and piles of money of all denominations. There were stacks of pennies sent by infants. Towers of 10p pieces sent by children. Skyscrapers of pound coins sent by teenagers. And bundles of notes sent by adults. They lay on the floor, on tables, on chairs, in the bath, in the sink. Wherever a space could be found.

To spice things up a little, Mrs. MacKenzie had started her own personal pile of notes. She was already planning what she was going to do with it. Unfortunately for her this had not gone unnoticed by Bill and Ben. 'Put it back,' growled the twins, pointing the taser at her menacingly. Mrs. MacKenzie reluctantly did as she was told, grumbling to herself as she did so.

After Johnny had telephoned him earlier, Ebenezer Dark had sprung into action like an excited middle-aged solicitor on his way to sue someone. Upon visiting the flat to take a look for himself at what was happening, he had quickly called Bill and Ben to come and help. They were overjoyed at the news and immediately put down the person they were beating up and hurried over wearing big cheesy grins on their faces.

They had greeted Johnny like a long-lost brother. Picking him up and giving him a great big bear hug before shooting extremely unpleasant looks in the direction of his parents. Like this:

|:-C

Next, Mr. Dark had called the bank and arranged for them to come and pick up the cash at regular intervals. Tenants of the council estate crowded around the heavily armed bank vans that appeared on the hour, every hour.

The money kept on coming. An avalanche of letters containing cash from people all over the world in all sorts of currencies. And the more the money arrived the more the press were willing to report it.

Mr. Dark took responsibility for counting the cash as the letters were delivered to the flat by harassed postmen and then dispatched to the bank by harassed security guards. The flat became a factory that converted letters into hard currency. And every hour Mr. Dark would gleefully report the running total to the hordes of reporters that surrounded the flat.

This figure was then broadcast live on the BBC home page and put up in lights in Piccadilly Circus. The whole world seemed gripped with Johnny Nothing fever. It was like Live Aid… Or Band Aid… Or Lucozade. It was like Comic Relief… Or Sports Relief… Or Acid Indigestion Relief.

Everybody in the world was looking down the side of the sofa for any loose change. Kids were giving up their sweet money. Burglars were robbing houses specifically so they could send the criminal proceeds to the Johnny Nothing fund. The government debated the cause in parliament and decided to increase taxes on the poor so that money could be handed to the fund. The Queen bought a cheaper dog food and donated the difference to Johnny. Everyone had gone Johnny Nothing crazy.

By 11.00 am that day Mr. Dark calculated that the total received was £80,000.
By 12.00 am that day Mr. Dark calculated that the total received was £170,000.
By 1.00 pm that day Mr. Dark calculated that the total received was £260,000.
By 2.00 pm that day Mr. Dark calculated that the total received was £260,000 (everybody had taken a break for lunch).
By 3.00 pm that day Mr. Dark calculated that the total received was £310,000.
By 4.00 pm that day Mr. Dark calculated that the total received was £380,000.
By 5.00 pm that day Mr. Dark calculated that the total received was £435,000.

By 6.00 pm that day Mr. Dark calculated that the total received was £435,000 (everybody had taken a break for dinner).

By 7.00 pm that day Mr. Dark calculated that the total received was £565,000.

By 8.00 pm that day Mr. Dark calculated that the total received was £605,000.

By 9.00 pm that day Mr. Dark calculated that the total received was £740,000.

By 10.00 pm that day Mr. Dark calculated that the total received was £740,000 (everybody had taken a break for supper).

By 11.00 pm that day Mr. Dark calculated that the total received was £860,000.

By 12.00 pm that day Mr. Dark calculated that the total received was £950,000.

By 1.00 am that day the MacKenzie family had gone to bed exhausted, Mr. Dark was asleep in the bath and the twins were snoring on the floor of the living room.

Chapter 30 – Rich

The next morning everyone woke up early. They were exhausted but pleasantly exhausted. Even Mrs. MacKenzie didn't moan too much.

They had coffee and listened to the crowds outside the flat chanting Johnny's name. He was now one of the most famous people in the country. Even more famous than Peter Andre or Susan Boyle or that bloke who used to be in Kajagoogoo from the 1980s. Soon the door would start knocking again and more letters would be delivered for them to open and sort.

But there was just enough time for a moment of reflection.

'I guess in all of this excitement some of you will have forgotten all about the reason we are here,' said Mr. Dark. 'So I should point out that today is the anniversary of Mr. Jake Marley's funeral. It's exactly a year ago that we all sat together in that church and listened to him speak.'

There was silence from the kitchen as the solicitor continued.

'Even a couple of months ago it would have seemed an impossible dream,' he said. 'But I think that if we all roll up our sleeves and work especially hard there's a very good chance that Johnny can get to the church by 3 o'clock with more than a £1 million in his possession.'

'Oh my gawd!' exclaimed Mrs. MacKenzie.

'Bloomin' nora,' said Bill and Ben in unison.

'Does that mean?' said Billy Mackenzie.

'Yes,' said Mr. Dark. 'It means that Johnny will have succeeded. He will have passed the task that Mr. Marley set him a year.'

Mr. Dark looked over at Johnny and winked. 'Lord knows how,' he said. 'But you've done it Johnny. Congratulations, my boy.'

Johnny smiled shyly and looked around at the rest of the adults in the room. At Bill and Ben, who were beaming with delight. At Billy MacKenzie, who seemed a little shell-shocked at the news. At his mother, who was dribbling slightly and rubbing her hands together at the prospect of all that money.

They set to work. Once more the front door became the conduit for thousands of cash donations from all over the world. Once more the flat was overwhelmed by piles and piles of the silver and green stuff. Once more envelopes came into the flat and once more money went out.

At 11.00 am the £1 million mark was finally passed. This landmark was greeted by a brief cheer from the room and then everyone went straight back to work. There was simply too much to do. The salty smell of sweat mingled with the dull aroma of copper.

At 1.30 pm Mr. Dark moved to the centre of the living room and instructed the others to stop sorting the money. He coughed a little before speaking, to let them know that what he was about to say was important: 'Hmm... Can I have everybody's attention,' he announced.

The others looked on.

'I think it's time that we thought about getting ourselves changed into something a little more presentable. We all need to clean ourselves up and get ready to leave for the church.'

The adults in the room simultaneously began to smile. They turned to look at the boy. Even Mrs. MacKenzie seemed happy for him.

Johnny put down the envelope he was holding and slowly got to his feet. 'I've been thinking about that,' he said gently.

There was silence in the room. Even the crowds outside the flat seemed to stop chanting for a moment or so.

Johnny put his hands to his face and cupped his cheeks. 'It's just that... Do we really need any more money?' he said finally.

There was a gasp of outrage from Mrs. MacKenzie. 'What are you talking about!' she growled.

'I mean, look at all this,' Johnny continued, pointing at the piles of money scattered around the flat. 'Isn't there enough here to last us a lifetime?'

'**NO! THERE! IS! NOT!**' exclaimed his mother with an exclamation mark after every word.

'Oh, do shut up and let the boy speak,' said Mr. Dark, a little surprised at his own boldness.

'I mean, what are we going to do with another £10 million?' said Johnny. 'Go to Harrods again?'

'Yes!' cried his mother.

'Or go on more of those stupid holidays...'

'Yes!' cried his mother.

'Or spend it on rubbishy gadgets...'

'Yes!' cried his father.

'Well I'm not,' said Johnny. 'And after all, it is MY money.'

'Yes it is your money,' smiled Mr. Dark. 'And what do you intend to do with it?'

'Give it back,' said Johnny.

'Give it back?' said Mrs. MacKenzie. 'What on earth do you mean?'

'Well look around you,' said Johnny. 'Look at where we live. Look at the people who live in the estate. Look at people everywhere who live in places like this. They've got nothing. All of us have got nothing.'

'You've got something, said Bill.

'That's right,' agreed Johnny. 'I've got something. And if I'm sensible I can try and make sure that other people have got something too.'

'Oh no!' cried his mother. 'Please don't tell me that you're going to give it all away again!'

'That's right,' said her son. 'I'm going to give it all away again.'

'Heaven help us all!' exclaimed Mrs. Mackenzie, sinking to the ground. 'I feel faint!'

'Only this time I'm going to do it right,' continued Johnny. 'No more giving the money away to any Tom, Dick or Harry. I'm going to be sensible. Will you help me this time Mr. Dark?'

Mr. Dark turned towards Johnny and smiled. 'Of course I will,' he replied. 'And I think it's about time you called me Ebenezer.'

'Bloody stupid name!' exclaimed Mrs. MacKenzie.

'I think it's a jolly good idea,' said Ebenezer Dark, ignoring the insult. 'But this time let's try to give the money away through the proper channels. We can set up a charity and give it to people who really need it.'

'Yeah…' said Ben. 'We can call it the Johnny Nothing Charity.'

'Or just the Nothing Charity,' said his brother.

'Or simply Nothing,' said Johnny Nothing.

'That's a nice name,' agreed Mr. Dark. 'Nothing can give something to those who have nothing. There's a nice feel to it.'

The three men looked at Johnny Nothing for a few moments.

'I hate to say this but I think you're doing the right thing,' said Bill.

'Yeah, I hate to give anything away for free but bruv's spot on,' agreed Ben.

Just like at the end of a really cheesy movie, the three men moved closer to the young boy. They placed their arms around him and finally gave him the group hug that I was talking about way back in Chapter 02.

Johnny was a millionaire again. He had somehow managed to recoup all of the money that his mother had frittered away. And more. But any sense of achievement would pale in comparison to what he was about to do next. Johnny MacKenzie, millionaire, was just about to turn himself back into Johnny Nothing.

But that didn't matter to Johnny. Because he felt like Johnny Everything.

'The boy's an idiot!' said his mother, lying on the floor and snivelling. 'A complete and utter buffoon!'

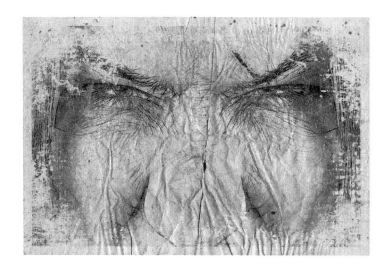

Epilogue

No one noticed as Felicity MacKenzie slipped quietly out of the flat. Ebenezer Dark was still talking as she quickly made her way out of the grounds of the council estate.

She was an unusual sight. She was wearing the clothes of a teenager but had the face of a middle-aged woman. The grey in her hair had been dyed blonde. Her nails were painted on like talons. Her clothing was far too big for her. She had lost so much weight over the past few months that they hung on her like rags on a Barbie doll on a break up from Ken with an eating disorder.

She walked fast, stopping only once to ask a passer-by the time. It was 2.45 pm. She had exactly fifteen minutes to get to the church. Felicity MacKenzie clutched the cash card tightly in her fingers and quickened her pace.

38807750R00110

Made in the USA
Charleston, SC
20 February 2015

The Wishing Starship

INTRO TO PHASE 5

/a_e/

Level 4+
Blue+

202129977

Helpful Hints for Reading at Home

The graphemes (written letters) and phonemes (units of sound) used throughout this series are aligned with Letters and Sounds. This offers a consistent approach to learning whether reading at home or in the classroom.

THIS BLUE+ BOOK BAND SERVES AS AN INTRODUCTION TO PHASE 5. EACH BOOK IN THIS BAND USES ALL PHONEMES LEARNED UP TO PHASE 4, WHILE INTRODUCING ONE PHASE 5 PHONEME. HERE IS A LIST OF PHONEMES FOR THIS PHASE, WITH THE NEW PHASE 5 PHONEME. AN EXAMPLE OF THE PRONUNCIATION CAN BE FOUND IN BRACKETS.

Phase 3			
j (jug)	v (van)	w (wet)	x (fox)
y (yellow)	z (zoo)	zz (buzz)	qu (quick)
ch (chip)	sh (shop)	th (thin/then)	ng (ring)
ai (rain)	ee (feet)	igh (night)	oa (boat)
oo (boot/look)	ar (farm)	or (for)	ur (hurt)
ow (cow)	oi (coin)	ear (dear)	air (fair)
ure (sure)	er (corner)		

New Phase 5 Phoneme	a_e (made, make, spades)

HERE ARE SOME WORDS WHICH YOUR CHILD MAY FIND TRICKY.

Phase 4 Tricky Words			
said	were	have	there
like	little	so	one
do	when	some	out
come	what		

TOP TIPS FOR HELPING YOUR CHILD TO READ:

• Allow children time to break down unfamiliar words into units of sound and then encourage children to string these sounds together to create the word.

• Encourage your child to point out any focus phonics when they are used.

• Read through the book more than once to grow confidence.

• Ask simple questions about the text to assess understanding.

• Encourage children to use illustrations as prompts.

INTRO TO PHASE 5
/a_e/

This book introduces the phoneme /a_e/ and is a Blue+ Level 4+ book band.

The Wishing Starship

Written by
John Wood

Illustrated by
Simona Hodonova

A big ship floats near the stars.
It is named The Wishing Starship.

When a wish is made, the shipmates
on The Wishing Starship make the
wish happen.

Zate hears the wish with an ear horn.
Then Zate jots down what the wish is.

Criss and Cross blend stardust and goo to make the wish. They mix it with spades.

Tank scrapes the wish up and tips it into a crate. Tank is a big snake.

Gabe checks that the wish is right.
Gabe shakes and shivers with glee.

Blake tapes the crate shut. Blake is little and is the same shape as a flower.

The ape shoots the wish out of a big gun.
Now the wish will happen.

Edna sweeps. "I am not as good as the rest of you," Edna sighs.

"You are just as good as the rest of the shipmates," the ape tells Edna.

"Can I have lunch now?" Blake moans.
"I cannot wait to have pink grapes."

"Wait for the lunch bell," the ape tells Blake. But Blake craves grapes now.

"I wish for a pink grape as big as a planet!" yells Blake.

The shipmates stop in shock. Blake made an unsafe wish. But they must make it happen!

Zate hears the wish. Criss and Cross blend the wish. They look afraid.

Tank scrapes the wish into a crate. Gabe checks the wish. Gabe shakes and shivers with fright.

Blake tapes shut the crate. The ape loads the wish into the gun and shoots.

A big pink grape appears and bumps the ship! The ship flips.

"I wish this was all back to how it was!" yells the ape.

The shipmates are all stuck. But Edna is not and Edna feels brave!

Edna hears. Edna blends. Edna scrapes. The shipmates are amazed at Edna's skill.

Edna checks. Edna tapes. Edna sweeps up a bit of mess. Edna shoots the big gun.

The big pink grape fades. The ship is
back to how it was.

"You did well," the ape tells Edna with a pat.
Edna grins.

The lunch bell rings.
"I wish I never run out of pink grapes,"
murmurs Gabe.

"No!" they yell.
But it is too late. They will have to make
this wish too!

The Wishing Starship

1) Who is shaped like a flower?

2) What is the last thing the shipmates do to make a wish happen?

   a) Shoot the wish out of a gun

   b) Kick the wish out the window

   c) Throw the wish in a bin

3) What does Blake wish for?

4) What job would you like to do on the ship?

5) What would you wish for from the shipmates?